Thomas Edgar Pemberton

John Hare, Comedian, 1865-1895

A Biography

Thomas Edgar Pemberton

John Hare, Comedian, 1865-1895
A Biography

ISBN/EAN: 9783744769044

Printed in Europe, USA, Canada, Australia, Japan

Cover: Foto ©Raphael Reischuk / pixelio.de

More available books at **www.hansebooks.com**

COMEDIAN

1865—1895

A BIOGRAPHY

BY

T. EDGAR PEMBERTON

AUTHOR OF "A MEMOIR OF E. A. SOTHERN," "THE LIFE AND WRITING
OF T. W. ROBERTSON," ETC. ETC.

LONDON

GEORGE ROUTLEDGE AND SONS Limited

BROADWAY, LUDGATE HILL

MANCHESTER AND NEW YORK

1895

CONTENTS.

CHAPTER I.

1865–1874.

THE PRINCE OF WALES'S THEATRE.

CHAPTER II.

1875–1879.

THE COURT THEATRE.

CHAPTER III.

1879–1888.

THE ST. JAMES'S THEATRE.

CHAPTER IV.

1889–1895.

THE GARRICK THEATRE.

CHAPTER V.

PERSONAL.

JOHN HARE

COMEDIAN

CHAPTER I.

1865–1874.

THE PRINCE OF WALES'S THEATRE.

Now that the inevitable has happened, and following the example of his famous brother and sister artists, Mr. John Hare has determined to cross the Atlantic and give American audiences a taste of his quality, the time has surely come when some record should be made of his thirty years' invaluable service to English dramatic art. Writing in the fast shortening days of 1895, my mind goes back to that memorable eleventh of November, 1865, when T. W. Robertson's often rejected comedy "Society" was, by those who believed in him, pluckily produced at the old Prince of Wales's Theatre, and a new era in the history of the English stage dawned.

All who take interest in things theatrical know the outcome of that famous first night. Let me, in connection with it, and as bearing directly on the leading figure in this little volume, quote the words of that true friend of the English stage,—Mr. Clement Scott,—at that time on the threshold of his distinguished career as a dramatic critic.

" There was," he writes, " a great gathering of the light literary division at the little theatre in Tottenham Court Road on the first night of Tom Robertson's new play. It was dear old Tom Hood, who was our leader then, who sounded the bugle, and the boys of the light brigade cheerfully answered the call of their chief. I remember that on that memorable night I stood—for there was no sitting room for us on such a great occasion—by the side of Tom Hood at the back of the dress circle. The days of stalls had not then arrived for me. Suddenly, as the play advanced, there

appeared on the stage what was then an ap-
parition. Bancroft had delighted us with his
cheery enthusiasm and boyish manner, for he
was the lover in this simple little play, well
dressed, and, for a wonder, natural. Think
what it was to see a bright, cheery, pleasant
young fellow playing the lover to a pretty girl
at the time when stage lovers were nearly all
sixty, and dressed like waiters at a penny ice
shop. But what astonished us even more than
the success of young Bancroft was the ap-
parition that I spoke of just now. A little,
delightful old gentleman came upon the stage
dressed in a long, beautifully-cut frock-coat,
bright-eyed, intelligent, with white hair that
seemed to grow naturally on the head—no
common clumsy wig with a black forehead
line—and with a voice so refined, so aristocratic,
that it was music to our ears. The part played
by Mr. Hare was, as we all know, insignificant.
All he had to do was to say nothing, and to go
perpetually to sleep. But how well he said
nothing; how naturally he went to sleep! We
could not analyse our youthful impression at the

time, but we knew instinctively that John Hare was an artist."

Those who remember the London stage in the early sixties will recognise that Mr. Scott's strictures concerning the penny ice shop waiter stage lovers were not one jot too severe. At the time when "Society" was produced, the English theatrical world,— a much smaller world than that of to-day,— was in a parlous state, and stood in as urgent need of reform as the great world outside it stood, as it stands to-day, and, I suppose, ever will stand. The smaller theatrical world is an easier thing to put in order, and that we may see how its mending came about, I may, perhaps, be permitted to point out what was being done at the other London theatres at the date of the production. Standing "Under the Clock" of the trustworthy "Times" I note that at Drury Lane Mr. Phelps, supported by Mr. Swinbourne, Mr. James Anderson, Miss Atkinson, Miss Rose Leclercq, and the now forgotten "Master Percy Roselle," were appearing in a destined to be short-lived production of

Shakespeare's "King John"; Sothern (who exactly four years previously, to the very day of the month, had made his London reputation as Lord Dundreary) was temporarily away from the Haymarket, and Mr. and Mrs. Charles Mathews were playing there with a company that included Mr. W. Farren, Mr. Chippendale, Mr. Compton, Mr. Charles Leclercq, Mr. Howe, Miss Nellie Moore, Miss Snowden (Mrs. Chippendale), Mrs. E. Fitzwilliam, Miss Louise Keeley and Miss Fanny Wright. At the Princess's Mr. Vining, Mr. G. Melville, Mr. T. Meade, Mr. Dominick Murray, Mr. S. Calhaem, Mr. J. G. Shore, Mr. G. Murray, Mr. R. Cathcart, Miss L. Moore, and Miss Katherine Rodgers were to be seen in Charles Reade's perennial "It's Never Too Late To Mend." At the Adelphi (here truly was a brilliant and exceptional attraction) America's great actor, Joseph Jefferson, was giving his inimitable impersonation of Rip Van Winkle, supported by an English company that included Mr. and Mrs. Billington, Mrs. Alfred Mellon, and

Mr. Paul Bedford. At the Lyceum, Fechter, with Mr. H. Widdicomb, Mr. S. Emery, Mr. C. Horsman, and Miss Elsworthy for his helpmates, was to be seen in a now forgotten drama called " The Watch Cry." The Olympic could boast of the services of Mr. Henry Neville, Mr. Horace Wigan, Mr. F. Younge, Mr. H. J. Montague, Mr. J. Maclean, Mr. R. Soutar, Miss Kate Terry, and Miss E. Farren; Miss Herbert, Mr. and Mrs. Frank Matthews, and Mr. Walter Lacy figured in the bills at the St. James's; and there were excellent burlesque companies at the Strand and the Royalty, the former boasting of such accomplished and popular comedians as Mr. J. D. Stoyle, Mr. David James, and Mr. Thomas Thorne. By the way, London's favourite comedian, Mr. J. L. Toole, must have been touring in the country, for his name is out of the programmes. Sir Henry Irving, it may be noted, was hard at work in provincial stock companies, preparing himself for his first London success, which was to be accomplished in 1866. No doubt much excellent acting was to be seen at these theatres, (what a small list it is when compared with that of to-day!) but most of the plays were poor ones, critics were dissatisfied, and theatre-goers had become alarmingly apathetic. Fechter had given the old-fashioned school a lesson in romantic acting, and Sothern had done equal service for comedy. The seeds of discontent had been sown ; following the lead of Oliver Twist, both critics and theatre-goers "asked for more," and they got it when the Bancroft reign commenced at the Prince of Wales's Theatre, when the delightful comedies of T. W. Robertson, adequately mounted and admirably acted, were produced, and when they recognised, as they immediately did, the unique gifts and perfected art of John Hare.

Says Mr. Clement Scott, "I don't suppose that before the curtain drew up on Robertson's 'Society,' anyone in London had heard a word about, or knew there was such a creature in existence, as John Hare. Before the curtain fell the young actor was famous, and everyone who had social or newspaper influence was talking about him."

Indeed Mr. Hare's stage experience is almost as unique as his genius, and his opportunity came to him just at the right time and just in the right way. Conscious of the power within him, and determined to try his fortune as an actor, he became in 1864 the pupil of Mr. Leigh Murray, and in 1865 he scored a genuine success on the London stage. Mr. Hare therefore can tell us no half humorous, half pitiful, stories of the rough days of the old provincial stock companies when on a starvation salary the would-be actor was expected to play some fifteen different and difficult parts in the course of a single week. We often are told of the good that these trying experiences did for subsequently famous actors, and no doubt in ninety-nine cases out of a hundred the contention holds good. But I believe I am right in saying that Mr. Hare's was the hundredth case,—the exception that proves the rule. If you want to put a point to a lancet you do not take it to the same grindstone that is to sharpen and polish an axe, and very probably too much disheartening and exhausting stock company work would have taken the edge and lustre off Mr. Hare's singularly delicate style. However that may be, it is certain that he did not want more tuition than he got.

Of his experiences in the brief pre-Prince of Wales's days of his theatrical career we learn something from Mr. and Mrs. Bancroft's delightful volume of reminiscences. We learn very little from Mr. Hare, for the innate modesty that is one of the great charms of his personal character is always wilfully and very wrongly telling him that his early experiences have little interest for the public. Mr. Bancroft has been kinder to us, and tells how, in 1864, and when he was a member of the stock company at the Prince of Wales's Theatre, Liverpool, he met " his oldest professional comrade, John Hare." " He was then," he says, " a young fellow of twenty, and had come to Liverpool accompanied by that once brilliant actor, Leigh Murray, whose pupil he had been, to make his first appearance on the stage. The friendship between Hare and myself soon became close, and there are few remembrances keener in my mind than frequent visits to his rooms, where Leigh Murray stayed with him for a time, and who, although suffering severely from asthma, and terribly crippled by rheumatism, was one of the most delightful companions I have ever known."

Before making his first appearance on the stage Mr. Hare had had very little experience as an amateur, and very few opportunities of theatre-going; but he was possessed with an ardent admiration for good acting, and all things connected with dramatic art. While reading with his tutor, the Rev. J. R. Blakiston, with a view to qualifying himself for the Civil Service, accident changed the whole course of his life. At the age of about nineteen he was invited by his friend Mr. Birkbeck to take part in some private theatricals given in his house at Settle, Yorkshire. The piece chosen (amateurs are nothing if not ambitious!) was " A Scrap of Paper," and the part assigned to him was that of a footman with one line to speak. During

the rehearsals it was obvious that no one connected with the entertainment had the slightest
idea of stage management or direction. " The
absence of this gift in others," Mr. Hare writes
me, " in some mysterious way developed it in
me, and before many days were over I found
myself directing the performance, and showing
the possession of the faculty which in later
years has done me such good service." The
night before the production of the play the
actor of the principal character, Prosper (the
" Colonel Blake" of the now well-known Hare-
and-Kendal version of the delightful comedy),
was taken ill, and Mr. Hare found himself
suddenly called upon to take his place. In order
to rehearse the part properly the next day, he
sat up all night to study it, and subsequently
played it with a success that brought about an
inevitable and severe attack of stage-fever.
Mr. Hare mentions this to me as an instance
of the quickness of his "study" when quite a
young fellow—the part being one of the longest
known in the range of comedy. It is interesting,
too, to note that it was the recollection of this

c

amateur performance that induced Mr. Hare years later to single out " A Scrap of Paper " for production at the Court Theatre.

Mr. Hare's little triumph as Prosper prompted a committee, organised in Settle for the purpose of giving an amateur dramatic performance in aid of the Lancashire Distress Fund, to offer him two parts—Beauséant in a burlesque on " The Lady of Lyons," and Box, in " Box and Cox." Again he was very successful, and by this time his mind was altogether unsettled for the work upon which he was avowedly engaged. Noticing this, Mr. Blakiston, who had seen these performances, with rare common sense, advised him to adopt the stage as a profession. At the tutor's intercession his uncle, who was also his guardian, waived his objections to his abandoning the career that had been mapped out for him, and Mr. Blakiston resigned his post in favour of Leigh Murray.

Of his dramatic master Mr. Hare has some interesting things to tell. " Leigh Murray," he says, "was at this time a man of about forty years of age, still very handsome, although almost a confirmed invalid, and continually suffering from asthma. In spite of this he possessed a beautiful voice, and his searching eyes and general charm of manner fascinated all who had the good fortune to know him. Apart from being a most accomplished and versatile actor, he was a most extraordinary mimic, and I have a very vivid recollection of his reading me the play of 'Richelieu' with exact imitations of the actors who played the principal characters —Macready, Ward, Elton, and others. Apropos of this I remember him telling me an amusing anecdote of Ward, the original Baradas of the play. Ward was a very bumptious man, with a didactic and ponderous utterance, and he had the reputation of being very thoughtless and extravagant. One winter, during the recess at Drury Lane, a recess that had been an unusually long one, and had drained to the very last extremity the resources of the actors out of engagements, Ward met Elton in Wellington Street. The friends shook hands; Elton enquired how Ward was, and Ward replied in his heavy manner : 'Dear boy, I am penniless, and haven't tasted food for the last three days.' This terrible admission shocked the good-hearted Elton, and taking from his pocket a purse which contained two half-sovereigns, he said : ' My poor old fellow ! I can't hear of a friend being in such distress as this ! I have only a sovereign myself, but here is half of it.' Ward, in a lordly and condescending way, pocketed the half-sovereign, said ' Thanks, dear boy,' as he waved his walking-stick to a passing Hansom : ' Cab !' and getting into the conveyance, drove away.

" Leigh Murray obtained me my first engagement at the Prince of Wales's Theatre, Liverpool, where he accompanied me to give me the benefit of his advice. Many a pleasant evening did I and the members of the company spend with him enjoying his rich fund of anecdote, which seemed to be inexhaustible. His memory was marvellous. He had a great love for and was a deep reader of poetry and the drama, and what he had once learnt he never forgot. Present at these little gatherings were S. B. Bancroft, Lionel Brough, W. Blakeley, and others who—beginners like myself—have since won fame and position on the London stage. It was in Liverpool that Leigh Murray first saw Sothern play David Garrick, and I remember how deeply he envied him the opportunity of creating that splendid part."

Mr. Hare's first professional appearance was made in a now forgotten piece entitled "A Woman of Business," in which, supporting Mr. J. L. Toole, who was fulfilling a starring engagement, he played the small part of a fop. This performance was attended by somewhat disastrous results, for towards the end of the little scene in which he was engaged Mr. Hare suddenly became the victim of stage fright, and utterly forgot every word he had to say. He was roused to a sense of his luckless position by the hoots and jeers of a derisive gallery, and fortunately these had an effect the reverse of what might have been expected. The young actor's anger was excited ; with his wrath his memory came back to him, and pulling himself together, he managed to get through the scene. But he was half heart-broken, and when he reached home he told Leigh Murray (who had been too ill to go to the theatre that night), that he had mistaken his vocation. Of course he was comforted and coached for his next fling with fortune. This was in a small part (the poet Lexicon) in "The Birthplace of Podgers," in which he again had the good luck to appear with Mr. Toole. Thanks, as he gratefully remembers, to the hints and encouragement of that genial comedian and ever kindly man, he gained confidence, and scored his first success, winning the laughter and applause of the audience, and (how sweet this always is to the young actor!) the recognition of the press.

"But best of all to me," says Mr. Hare, "was the approval of my old friend Toole. This early meeting with him was the commencement of a friendship which has increased and lasted down to the present time."

Mr. Hare's next good fairy was the late E. A. Sothern who, pleased with his performance of the stammering Jones in "David Garrick," cast him for a somewhat important part in his new play, "The Woman in Mauve."

This was to be produced in Liverpool upon the return of Sothern from an engagement which he had to fulfil in Manchester, and the piece was to be rehearsed during his absence by a deputy. Mr. Hare learnt subsequently that his manner of rehearsing the part gave the greatest alarm to the manager, Mr. Henderson, who thought him far too inexperienced to play it. As a matter of consequence letters and telegrams were continually going between Liverpool and Manchester urging Sothern to make an alteration in the cast, and to give the part to the recognised low comedian of the theatre. Sothern, however, was steadfast, and insisted that the young actor, whose talent he had recognised, should have his chance. His judgment was correct, and on the first night, at the end of the second act, he led his protégé before the curtain in graceful acknowledgment of the fact that in the scene that had just called forth applause honours had been fairly divided.

This episode receiving notice at the hands of some of the London critics, encouraged Mr. Hare to hope for an immediate engagement in town, and when he had been seen successfully acting in H. J. Byron's little piece called " An Old Story," by the author and Miss Marie Wilton, and they had said many kindly and encouraging things of his perform- ance, visions of an offer from the new manage- ment of the Prince of Wales's Theatre tantalised him.

That offer, however, did not (offers rarely do) spontaneously come, and it was not until he had confided his aspirations and troubles to John Clarke, who was engaged as a leading member of the new London company, that, following his friend's advice, he boldly "wrote in," as actors have it, and offered his services, prepared to "do anything he was told, play any part that was offered him, and be grateful for any salary he could get." The result of this plucky policy was an engagement at £2 a week, plus a fixed resolve to make the most of any opportunity that might come in his way.

An early Liverpool performance of Mr. Hare's in company with Mr. Bancroft was that of Pinch (the " schoolmaster and conjuror ") in a production of Shakespeare's "Comedy of Errors," in which Mr. Bancroft appeared as Antipholus of Syracuse, and the brothers Charles and Harry Webb played the two Dromios. In consequence of the extraordinary likeness existing between these two comedians, this was, in the days of 1864, a very popular entertainment, and in connection with it I may, perhaps, be permitted to tell a story that deserves a place in the "Curiosities of Criticism." On one occasion when the Webbs were engaged to appear as the Dromios at a provincial theatre, Charles missed his train and telegraphed to Harry that he could not appear on the stage until about the time that the curtain might be expected to fall. Now it will be remembered that Dromio of Ephesus does not meet Dromio of Syracuse until the final scene of the play, and, grasping the situation as a true actor should, Harry Webb played the two parts all through the piece,— took care that the waits between the acts were as long as the audience would allow them, and at the end of the comedy,—just at the right moment,—had the satisfaction of standing face to face with quickly dressed and hastily made-up brother Charles. This, of course, was no very great achievement; the pith of my story lies in the fact that in the next day's local newspaper, the astute critic sneered at the preposterous notion of the brothers *considering themselves like each other.* " A mere tyro," he majestically declared, "could at any moment have seen which of the two occupied the stage!"

I do not suppose that Mr. Hare could make much of Pinch; but as one of his few Shake-spearean impersonations, his appearance in the part is worthy of record. Mr. Bancroft tells us that he " presented a very quaint figure," and also noted that when the Webbs appeared as Dubosc and Lesurques in " The Courier of Lyons " (" The Lyons Mail " of Sir Henry Irving's Lyceum repertory), " Hare gave the first sign of his power in the art of making-up in a small part of a very old man."

When Sothern came to Liverpool with his second great success, " David Garrick," with Lionel Brough for his Squire Chevy, Hare, as we have seen, played the poor and ridiculous part of the stuttering Jones,—one of Alderman Ingot's impossible guests,—and when a little later on the clever but ill-starred "Woman in Mauve" of Watts Phillips was produced, Sothern entrusted him with the character of the ex-policeman, subsequently played during the very brief run of the piece at the Haymarket by Mr. Compton.

Writing of this play and its tentative production, Watts Phillips, who was not present, said :

"It appears my 'Woman in Mauve' has been a most *extraordinary* success in Liverpool. They wanted originality, and they have got it, —for the critiques declare that 'such a piece has never been seen before on the English stage,'— and Sothern says that the astonishment and enthusiasm were wonderful. It will be produced in about six weeks at the Haymarket, and they expect it will take London by storm. We shall see!"

Alas for the fond hopes of the ever sanguine Sothern, and the often disappointed author, they *did* see, and all that is now remembered of a whimsically conceived and cleverly written but unsuccessful play, is Mr. Bancroft's droll anecdote of one of Hare's first appearances as ex-constable Beetles.

" The leading characters in the second act," he says, " were joining in the chorus to a song sung by Sothern, Hare beating time with a telescope, which he used throughout the play as a kind of memory of his former truncheon. One night the audience roared with laughter louder and louder at each successive verse; the actors doubled their exertions,—Hare especially, who attributed part of their enjoyment to the vigorous use of his impromptu *bâton*—when Sothern, who was next to him, suddenly discovered that various articles of costume, used by Hare as padding, were one by one emerging from beneath his coat, and forming an eccentric looking little heap upon the stage. The audience roared louder than ever; Hare beating time with renewed fierceness, when Sothern whispered : 'Never mind, old fellow; don't take any notice; don't look down !' Of course Hare did look down at once; he saw what had happened, and bolted in confusion, leaving us to finish the scene as best we could without him."

Mr. Bancroft further makes mention of a performance of " Money," in which he played Captain Dudley Smooth, and Mr. Hare was cast for the subordinate part of the irascible old member of the club whose time is passed in calling for the snuff-box. No doubt this production was recalled by the Sir Frederick Blount and Sir John Vesey at the famous revival of Lord Lytton's comedy at the Prince of Wales's Theatre in 1872.

We now clearly understand how it came about that when Mr. Bancroft became a prominent member of Miss Marie Wilton and Mr. H. J. Byron's London Company he was soon followed by his old Liverpool comrade, Mr. Hare, whose first appearance on the metropolitan boards was made at the Prince of Wales's Theatre on September 25, 1865, as the landlord Short in the well known " Naval Engagements." " Byron," says Mr. Bancroft, " would drag in a joke, and at rehearsal one day remarked to Hare : 'So wise to appear first of all in a part suited to you. Short figure, short name, short part; the critics will say: ' Mr. Hare, a clever young actor, made his first bow to a London audience, and was most excellent; in short, perfect.' ' Yes,' said Mr. Hare; ' but what will happen if they don't like me ?' ' We'll rechristen the piece " Short *Engagements*." ' "

Though the time and the opportunity for making his great mark had not yet arrived, the " in short, perfect " prophecy was very near the mark, and, as we all know, the engagement became a very long one.

As we have seen, lasting success came with his unique and almost startling performance of Lord Ptarmigant in T. W. Robertson's " Society," on November 11 of the same year. This was at once appreciated by the critics and the public, and the fame of the actor was firmly established. Following the custom of those days the bill was strengthened at Christmas by the production of a burlesque. This was entitled " Little Don Giovanni," and was from the pen of Mr. H. J. Byron. In it Miss Marie Wilton appeared as the Don (how delightful she was in such characters will never be forgotten by old playgoers!) and, probably very much against his will, Mr. Hare figured as Zerlina. It was almost the last piece of its class ever produced at the theatre. Henceforth the resources of this admirable company were to be very properly devoted to pure comedy.

May 5, 1866, witnessed the production of H. J. Byron's comedy "A Hundred Thousand Pounds," in which Mr. Hare, with distinct success, played the character of Mr. Fluker. It is a pleasant piece, and is still very popular with amateurs, but although it advanced Mr. Hare's position on the London stage it did not otherwise greatly add to the acting reputation of any one of those who first appeared in it.

T. W. Robertson's next comedy at the Prince of Wales's Theatre was "Ours," the play in which the author's great love of and sympathy with soldiers first showed itself. It had its trial trip at the Prince of Wales's Theatre, Liverpool, and at the first reading some disappointment was expressed by those who were to appear in it, Mr. John Hare especially feeling that the part of Prince Perovsky (subsequently one of his notable successes) was unsuited to him. By this time he knew his own value, and was naturally anxious with regard to new ventures, but when Robertson told him that if he would accept the part he should regard it in the light of a personal favour, he readily acceded. On September 15, 1866, the charming play was presented in London, and at once made its mark. While the acting of all concerned was deservedly praised, it was clearly pointed out that Mr. Hare had made another distinct step forward, and that no more complete impersonation had been for some time seen, than his embodiment of the Russian Prince, characterized by the highest polish and the utmost refinement of speech and manner.

It was during this original run of "Ours," that H.R.H. the Prince of Wales sent for Mr. Hare during the performance, and graciously complimented him on his impersonation of the Russian Prince. Since that time not a year has passed without his having received some mark of the Prince's kindness and appreciation of work well done. He has seen nearly every play that Mr. Hare has produced or appeared in, and has never failed to express his pleasure. "Often," says Mr. Hare, "I have had the advantage of his shrewd and kindly judgment, and I believe him to be one of the best, as he is one of the most sympathetic of critics." On the occasion of this first introduction to the Prince, Mr. Hare had good cause to be struck by his well-known minute observation of detail. His uniform as the Russian General was complete in every detail (for the taking of pains in such matters Mr. Hare is without a rival), but, thinking that no one in front would be much concerned about the authenticity of his decorations, he allowed himself to wear a rather mixed lot, among them being the order of a freemason. This the Prince had noticed through his glasses, and when he met Mr. Hare he at once condemned the entire display as preposterous and absurd. The error was immediately rectified, but the little story shows how quickly the Prince detects the slightest inaccuracy in dress and appropriate decoration.

D

On the other hand, he is the first to recognize correctness.

What a contrast was there between Prince Perovsky and the next character our actor was called upon to play! what a surprising change from the haughty, high-minded, aristocratic Russian Prince, to that of Sam Gerridge, the commonplace, jealous, and plebeian little tradesman of the Borough Road, who informs all and sundry that he has succeeded to the business of the late Mr. Binks, and that " Bell-'anging, gas-fittin', plumbin', and glazin' would be carried on as usual!"

When, on April 6, 1867, Robertson's masterpiece was produced at the Prince of Wales's Theatre, Mr. Hare's Sam Gerridge was one of the surprises and the triumphs of a delightful and memorable evening. Mr. Clement Scott attributes much of this success to the dramatist. "What a keen observer," he says, " was Tom Robertson! He saw Hare clearly and distinctly as Lord Ptarmigant; but he saw him also, sharp, decisive, cockney to the backbone, as Sam Gerridge, the gas-fitter."

Robertson would, no doubt, have given the praise to the actor, and the truth of the matter is that it was a case of mutual obligation.

Writing of this production a leading critic said : " The most natural and powerful character in the play is the drunken father, a selfish sot, partly self-deluded, partly a humbug "—by the way Mr. Hare has sometimes said that he would play Eccles. Why does he not do it ?— " Next to him stands the other and the real working man, a mechanic whose flow of speech is not great, but who makes his presence felt by judicious 'business.' Mr. Hare is so refined and perfect an actor, so true an observer of life, that we were not surprised to find him made up a sharp, wiry, veritable working man who might have stepped out of any carpenter's shop in England. The scene in which he reads to his 'intended' the trade circular he has just composed is the most exquisite and unforced bit of comedy we have seen for years."

It was a performance that had a firm hold on the public. On April 13, 1883, when, at the Haymarket Theatre, " Caste " was played for

the last time under the famous Bancroft
management (by the way, it was during the
first run of " Caste " that Marie Wilton became
Mrs. Bancroft), Mr. Hare came over from the
St. James's Theatre to play his old part to the
Captain Hawtree and Polly Eccles of his
former manager. " That evening," says Mrs.
Bancroft, " will long be remembered by us, and
is not likely to fade easily from the memory of
anyone present. It was apparent, directly the
curtain rose, that the audience was exceptional,
and that some strange magnetic influence
affected both auditor and actor. The reception
of all the familiar characters was very pro-
longed, while that of Mr. Hare, the moment
he appeared as Sam Gerridge, and of ourselves,
no other word will so express the demonstration
as ' affection '."

Playgoers who remember these brilliant impersonations will agree with me in saying that
this is exactly the right word used in the right
place. To Mr. Hare the evening was made
doubly memorable by the presentation to him
by the Bancrofts of a beautiful silver vase.

On December 21, 1867, "Caste" was succeeded at the Prince of Wales's by Dion
Boucicault's five-act comedy, entitled "How She
Loves Him." Mr. Hare's character was that of
Mr. Nettletop (divorced from his wife), but
though the piece had proved attractive in
America it failed to please in London, and was
soon forgotten. As an afterpiece (in those
days audiences were exacting enough to expect
an afterpiece) Maddison Morton's immortal
"Box and Cox" was staged, with the following
cast : Box, Mr. George Honey ; Cox, Mr.
Hare ; Mrs. Bouncer, Mrs. Leigh Murray.
Those who saw this matchless piece of farce
acting by three great artists will never forget it.

On Saturday, February 15, 1868, Robertson's
new comedy "Play" was produced. It was, no
doubt, the weakest of the famous series con-
tributed by him to the Bancroft *régime*, but in
it Mr. Hare was able to score in a curiously
original stage study. Speaking of the Hon.
Bruce Fanquehere, the *Times* critic said :
"His morals are somewhat lax, but his prin-
ciples, when a point of honour is concerned, are

sound, and when interest does not decidedly pull the wrong way he is an earnest though cool advocate on the side of right. Mr. Hare, always ready to seize on exceptional peculiarities of character, is the very man to perform the character, and the figure he presents with thin legs, imperturbable demeanour, and a dress which, though plain, borders on the 'slangy,' is entirely new to the stage." Of the same performance Mr. Dutton Cook says : " In the part of the Hon. Bruce Fanquehere, Mr. Hare finds an opportunity for presenting the public with another specimen of his skill in character painting. Mr. Bruce, with all his viciousness and utter want of principle, is yet master of a certain well-bred gentlemanly manner which Mr. Hare is heedful never to lose sight of, and to keep constantly under the notice of the audience."

But " Play " was not a second " Ours " or " Caste," and on December 12, 1868, " Tame Cats," an original comedy by Edmund Yates, was brought out. This proved one of those saddest of sad things—a first-night failure. Sad, that is to say, to those who think with me.

Mr. Bancroft tells us that " cat-calls and feline sounds of many kinds followed the final fall of the curtain, and we felt the play was doomed." Even to read of such a brutal demonstration as this, and of such wanton insults offered to a clever writer and an exceptional company of actors and actresses, makes the blood of the honest playgoer boil. And yet this sort of thing is still, to the disgrace of the English stage, going on. I wonder what sort of people these first-night hissers, and hooters, and cat-callers are ? I suppose it is exceedingly unlikely that they are familiar with the words of George Eliot, or they would remember that that great writer said : " Failure after perseverance is much grander than never to have a striving good enough to be called a failure." I am quite certain that the great majority of theatre-goers will agree with me when I say that I would far rather wake up on the morning following one of these vulgar and unseemly outrages to find myself critically condemned as an unsuccessful actor or author, than to know that I had been guilty of taking even the smallest part in an ill-bred and cruel display of temper. It is true that, years afterwards, Edmund Yates said that " Tame Cats" was poor stuff and deserved its fate, but neither he nor the Prince of Wales's company thought so at the time of its production, and if they mutually made a mistake they deserved commiseration and not insult.

In connection with this ill-fated venture Mr. Bancroft says : " Hare had to appear as a shabby and disreputable creature who was a returned convict : he was, as usual, immensely excited about his 'get-up,' which was mutually discussed over one of the many delightful dinners of those early days. I remember an amusing incident of his hunting in all sorts of back streets for some characteristic clothes, and after walking round and round a strange man who wore a very odd-looking hat, which Hare thought priceless, at last striking a bargain for its purchase with the bewildered owner, and carrying it off in triumph with some horrible rags of garments which had to be well baked in an oven before they could be worn."

On January 16, 1869, Robertson's "School," partly founded on the German play " Aschenbrödel" of Roderich Benedix, was produced with such complete success that the former disappointment was speedily forgotten. In this Mrs. Bancroft was delightful in that which she has since admitted to be her favourite part, Naomi Tighe ; Mr. Bancroft was most happily fitted as Jack Poyntz ; and as the cosmeticised and decrepit Beau Farintosh Mr. Hare made another distinct mark.

Of this performance the critic of the *Daily Telegraph* said : "Whatever part Mr. Hare undertakes we may be quite assured the utmost amount of pains will be bestowed on every detail ; and this most creditable characteristic of the actor is especially to be noticed in his latest assumption. Beau Farintosh, who might have been a young 'buck' in the days of the Regency, but who is now only a padded old man striving to repair the ravages of nature by the appliances of art, must be ranked the very best of Mr. Hare's impersonations. The carefully made-up face, in which the wrinkles are effaced by the plastering of cosmetics, the affected jaunty air of youth contrasting with the unavoidable feeble gait, and the blundering short-sightedness of which he seems to be so amusingly unconscious, are admirably exhibited. An effective contrast is also produced when he no longer affects to conceal the years he has attained ; and when, clasping his long-sought grandchild to his arms with emotions which overpower his utterance, the old beau reappears as a grey-headed old gentleman, inspiring reverence instead of ridicule. The burst of pathos which accompanies this wholesome change favourably displays the power of the actor in a strong situation."

In September, 1891, Mr. Hare revived "School" at the Garrick Theatre, but to the great regret of playgoers did not reappear as the whimsical but warm-hearted old beau. The cast was, however, in many respects an interesting one. Mr. H. B. Irving, the son of Sir Henry Irving, appeared as Lord Beaufoy ; Mr. Hare's son, Gilbert Hare, was the Mr. Krux ; Mr. C. W. Garthorne, Mr. Kendal's brother, the Jack Poyntz ; Miss Fanny Robertson, the sister of the dramatist and of Mrs. Kendal, the Mrs. Sutcliffe ; and Miss Kate Rorke, who was one of the schoolgirls in the Haymarket revival of the play under the Bancroft reign, the Bella. The part of Beau Farintosh was entrusted to that excellent character actor Mr. Mackintosh.

On April 23, 1870, the Bancrofts produced " M.P.," the last of the series of delightful comedies that poor Robertson wrote for the perfectly organised little company that he understood so well. He was in failing health when he wrote it (indeed the end of it was dictated by him from his bed of sickness), he was unable to attend the rehearsals, and, as a matter of course, the work suffered. But good acting saved it, and in the finely drawn character of Dunscombe Dunscombe Mr. Hare scored another notable success.

" Mr. Hare," said a leading critic, speaking of this performance, " is the most finished actor of old men that our stage has had since the late William Farren if we except Mr. Alfred Wigan,

who might, and no doubt will, be pre-eminent
in this line of business whenever he takes to it.
As it is, Mr. Hare has no rival in our theatres
at this moment.   The one new incident of the
comedy, and the best part intrinsically of
Mr. Robertson's piece, is the scene of the sale
by auction in Dunscombe Hall, which may have
been suggested by the late R. Martineau's impressive picture of 'The Last Day in the Old
House,' but on which as well Mr. Robertson is
to be congratulated, both for his choice and
his treatment of the incident, as his actors—
Mr. Hare more particularly—for their perfect
realization of the author's intention.   We remember no more natural and touching passage
of mingled comedy and pathos than the best
part of this third act, and it alone would have
secured the success of the piece.   Mr. Hare's
performance, in conception and execution, was
the gem of the piece.   The scene in which the
old squire resents Piers's " (this was the part so
perfectly played by Mr. Bancroft) "charge, and
that which follows when he listens to the voice
of the auctioneer knocking down his ancestral

pictures, rises to the highest rank of acting in contemporary comedy. Throughout, his performance illustrated admirably a truth very important to dramatists and actors, namely, how wide and unoccupied a field there is for effective impersonation, even in the studiously unmasked and reticent manners of contemporary life, and among the class most careful to mask emotion and put the curb on all expression of it."

Notwithstanding this great and thoroughly artistic success, the popular impersonator of Dunscombe Dunscombe was by this time growing a little restless. " Held down, as it were, by long runs," says Mr. Bancroft, " Mr. Hare asked our permission, which was at once accorded, to give a special *matinée* at the Princess's Theatre." As an actor, it may here be noted, Mr. Hare has always disliked long runs, maintaining that after some fifty nights in one character the actor becomes mechanical in his part. Whether as a manager he holds precisely the same views is more than I can say. The cast of the Princess's *matinée* is worth quoting here, for it shows how, at even this comparatively early stage of the actor's career, he was esteemed by the flower of the theatrical profession. The programme commenced with the good old farce of "The Bengal Tiger," in which Mr. and Mrs. Alfred Wigan acted; and this was followed by "London Assurance," in which Mr. Hare as Sir Harcourt Courtly was supported by Mr. H. J. Montague as Charles Courtly, Mr. Addison as Max Harkaway, Mr. Bancroft as Dazzle, Mr. Buckstone as Dolly Spanker, Mr. J. L. Toole as Mark Meddle, Mr. John Clayton as Cool, Mr. C. Collette as Solomon Isaacs, Mrs. Bancroft as Lady Gay Spanker, Miss Carlotta Addison as Grace Harkaway, and Miss Nellie Farren as Pert. If with such a cast as this "London Assurance" could be revived to-day what crowded houses it would draw! Alas! it took place as long ago as 1870, and was then "for one afternoon only." Another attraction of that memorable afternoon was that Arthur Sullivan (he was not "Sir Arthur" in those days) and Frederick Clay played the piano between the acts.

The next important production at the Prince of Wales's Theatre was the notable revival of Lord Lytton's comedy " Money." It gained new life for a neglected and supposed to be (from an actor's point of view) " unlucky " play, and was a bright feather in the managerial cap. As Sir John Vesey Mr. Hare met with a new occasion for exhibiting his skill in histrionic portraiture. With a suffused face, white hair and whiskers, a restless pomposity of manner, and a plausible geniality that only gave way when selfishness became urgent, " Stingy Jack " in Mr. Hare's hands acquired a position of unusual prominence in the comedy. The representation was complete in every respect, and marked by particular ingenuity in the contrivance of by-play, and what is called " stage business."

In Wilkie Collins's powerful play " Man and Wife " (by the way, Mr. Hare first brought this work to the notice of the Bancrofts) he appeared as Sir Patrick Lundie, and was enabled to produce another of his now established portraitures of a shrewd, sarcastic, and yet kindly elderly gentleman.

April 1874, witnessed that elaborate and in many espects remarkable revival of "The School for Scandal" that will always have its place in the story of the English stage, and in which Mr. Hare was the Sir Peter Teazle. Concerning this impersonation I shall once more make so bold as to quote the critic of the *Daily Telegraph*. "How loyally and well," he says, "Mr. Hare would assist such a performance we all know, and how the performance was in itself brought into relief by Mr. Hare's good taste we must all be convinced. Without such a Sir Peter, who refines everything to a nicety, who remembers the tone and character of the old English gentleman, and studiously forgets the coarseness, and we may add the grossness, which has been attached to the character by tradition, how much less expression would have been obtained by the great scene with Lady Teazle! Surely a young actor can play Sir Peter Teazle without being obstinately compared with such geniuses as are identified with the character, and we may well congratulate Mr. Hare in successfully passing through a most harassing and almost overwhelming ordeal. It is difficult to shake the conviction of anyone, and with old playgoers old memories are necessarily dear ; but it will be gratefully remembered that in Sir Peter Teazle Mr. Hare, true to his art, discarded those coarse effects which are so telling, and, remembering his own standard and outlook of the character, played it, with evenness and finish, and like a refined and well-bred gentleman."

"It was at this time," writes Mr. Bancroft, " that our company suffered a great loss in the departure of its oldest and most valued member, John Hare. Wisely enough, for there was ample room for two such theatres as the then Prince of Wales's in friendly rivalry, he had for some time entertained ideas of commencing management on his own account ; how wisely has been proved by the splendid record of his work in that direction.

"When 'The School for Scandal' was withdrawn Hare left us, Sir Peter Teazle being the last part he played under our management ; but time has not weakened our remembrance of his

E

valued services and the great aid he gave to the Robertson comedies, with which his name must always be associated, or, I rejoice to add, altered our friendship. He and I had dressed in the same room together for years, those years being, at least on my part, the happiest of my life, for they began when I was twenty-four and ended when I was thirty-three. I know I can claim to be his oldest theatrical friend, and I don't suppose he was surprised that the little dressing-room knew me no more, for the next night I found a lonely corner somewhere else."

CHAPTER II.

THE COURT THEATRE.

THE time was certainly ripe for the organ-
ization of a new high-class company of
comedians when, on March 13, 1875, Mr. Hare
opened the Court Theatre (the parent of the
existing Court Theatre) in Sloane Square,
Chelsea. Buckstone's famous Haymarket company had been disbanded, and this enabled him
to secure the services of Mrs. Kendal (who
still figured in the programmes as Miss Madge
Robertson) and Mr. Kendal, and other engagements were made with Mrs. Gaston Murray
(then playing as Miss Hughes), Miss Amy
Fawsitt, Miss Bessie Hollingshead, Miss Mary
Rorke, Mr. R. Cathcart, Mr. H. Kemble, Mr.
Charles Kelly, and Mr. John Clayton; in all
truth a goodly company. The pretty little

E 2

playhouse was tastefully decorated—at his own wish Mr. Val Prinsep painted a new act-drop, which was equally novel, tasteful, and excellent —and the opening night went off with great *éclat.*

The chief attraction was " Lady Flora," a new and original four-act comedy by Mr. Charles Coghlan, who since the production of " M.P." had been a very prominent member of the Prince of Wales's Company. It was a pleasant play of the Robertsonian school, written with a sprightliness and a measure of tenderness, and it proved both attractive and amusing. Once more perfectly made-up, Mr. Hare gave a fine and highly finished picture of a French Duke resident in England, playing throughout with his known ease and tact; Mrs. Kendal was charming as Lady Flora; Mr. Kendal acted admirably in rather a thankless part; Mr. John Clayton also made his mark; and Mr. Kelly scored heavily as a good-natured English nobleman, brusque in manner but warm in heart. Altogether Mr. Hare's best friends could not have wished him a better " send-off."

On June 12, "Lady Flora" was succeeded by Mr. Hamilton Aïdé's interesting four-act comedy-drama " A Nine Days' Wonder," in which Mr. Hare appeared as an elderly widower, Mr. Vavasour by name, who for the proverbial " nine days " is in danger of becoming enmeshed in the matrimonial snares of Mrs. Fitzroy (a part superbly rendered by Mrs. Kendal), who a quarter of a century previously had refused his hand. Mr. Hare's performance had all the minute realism of his well-known method, and was equally picturesque and effective.

With Mr. and Mrs. Kendal fresh from their Haymarket triumphs in " The Palace of Truth," " Pygmalion and Galatea," and " The Wicked World," as the leading members of his company, it was but natural that Mr. Hare should wish to produce one of those fascinating stage fairy stories in which Mr. Gilbert had found convenient vehicles for his piquant fun and trenchant satire. Accordingly, on December 9, he staged that delightful writer's " Broken Hearts " with Mrs. Kendal as Lady Hilda, Mr. Kendal as

Prince Florian, and Mr. G. W. Anson as the dwarf—Mousta—the character in which he made his first great London success. Possibly this was the part designed by the author for Mr. Hare, but, be that as it may, he elected not to appear in the piece. Indeed, now that he had become his own manager he seemed almost to wish to efface himself as an actor. This, no doubt, was following out his theory that the *ideal* theatrical manager should be one who, whilst possessing the best artistic knowledge and thorough command over his company, is self-sacrificing enough not to act himself.

But, luckily for dramatic art, his audiences not only wanted to see him on the stage, but let him know it, and he had to respond to their call.

It was on January 8, 1876, that Mr. Hare appeared for the first time as Lord Kilclare in Mr. Coghlan's adaptation from the French, entitled " A Quiet Rubber," and achieved one of his greatest and most lasting stage triumphs. The success was won in the face of great difficulty. Barely five years had elapsed since Mons. Lesueur had visited London and appeared at the Lyceum in " La Partie de Piquet," the French original of Mr. Coghlan's English play, and theatre-goers were still talking of the masterly presentation given by that admirable artist of the hero of the little piece, a member of an old-fashioned aristocracy, nurtured in prejudice and delusions which even the earthquake shock of revolution could not overthrow. Everyone was saying not only that the piece could not be Anglicised, but that neither Mr. Hare nor any other English comedian could give an adequate rendering of this extraordinarily subtle character. · How these difficulties were cleverly overcome by the adapter, and absolutely vanquished by the actor, is now a matter of theatrical history. For nearly twenty years Lord Kilclare, as impersonated by Mr. Hare, has held his own upon the boards, and, indeed, there is no more popular figure on the stage than the proud and irascible old nobleman in the familiar high collars and brown coat with brass buttons. The part proved itself to be peculiarly adapted to Mr. Hare's method. A little fire of manner

that in the eyes of some critics had occasionally
detracted from the value of his pictures of age,
was here in keeping, and gave added effect to
the haughty insolence which is hidden behind
elaborate and ostentatious courtesy.   If he had
never done anything else, Mr. Hare's Lord
Kilclare would ever keep his memory green.
It is one of those unique impersonations that
English play-goers love to see over and over
again.

The March of the same year witnessed the
first production at the Court Theatre of Mr. J.
Palgrave Simpson's revised adaptation of
Sardou's "Les Pattes de Mouche," still happily
called "A Scrap of Paper." We have seen
how as an amateur Mr. Hare had appeared in
and been attracted to this remarkably clever
comedy.   It was first produced on the English
stage with Mr. and Mrs. Alfred Wigan in the
parts destined to become so famous in the
hands of Mr. and Mrs. Kendal, but on that
occasion was merely a *succès d'estime*.   This,
Mr. Hare felt, was mainly due to the fact that
Mrs. Alfred Wigan, although perfectly artistic

in all she did, was at the time it fell in her way
too old for the part of the vivacious and
fascinating heroine. Her performance was full
of ability, but it had lacked " charm." In Mrs.
Kendal's clever hands he felt certain that this
difficult character would from every point of
view be perfectly safe; and the result proved
the correctness of his judgment. "A Scrap of
Paper" was an immediate and enormous
success at the Court Theatre, and was subsequently one of the most brilliant revivals of
the Hare and Kendal management at the
St. James's. It still proves—and as long as
they go on playing it is likely to prove—one of
the most attractive and popular items of Mr.
and Mrs. Kendal's repertory. In the first
production of the play under his management
Mr. Hare, for the sake, presumably, of showing
his versatility, elected to appear in the boy's
part, Archie Hamilton. Wonderfully made-up,
and presenting an absolutely youthful appearance, he played with a brightness of style that
was at once captivating and convincing. I
remember on one occasion seeing Mr. Hare

follow up this daring and dashing performance
with an appearance as the infirm old Lord
Kilclare, and I have reason to know that a
number of people in the theatre could not be
convinced that the same actor had played the
two parts.

In later productions of " A Scrap of Paper "
Mr. Hare appeared as the eccentric old ento-
mologist, Dr. Penguin, and in wonderful
suggestions about the eyebrows and whiskers
conveyed the idea that he had become so
absorbed in his hobby that he was getting to
look like one of his treasured specimens.

After the first run of the play Mr. and Mrs.
Kendal left the Court Theatre to fulfil an
engagement with the Bancrofts at the Prince of
Wales's, and, fortifying his company by the
important engagement of Miss Ellen Terry,
Mr. Hare produced, on November 4, 1876, a
new three-act comedy, by Mr. Coghlan, called
" Brothers." It was a brightly written play,
and the acting had the *ensemble* that Mr. Hare
had striven so hard and so successfully to
impart, but it did not " draw the town," and it

was very speedily succeeded by a revival of
Messrs. Tom Taylor and A. W. Dubourg's
charming comedy " New Men and Old Acres,"
in which Miss Ellen Terry played the part
created by Mrs. Kendal on the original production of the piece at the Haymarket, and Mr.
Hare followed Mr. Chippendale as Vavasour.
By all concerned this was so beautifully acted—
and by Mr. Hare so perfectly stage-managed—
that solid and lasting success was assured.
The good work that was being done was generously recognised, and the critical *Athenæum*
spoke for the public when it said : " Without
going to the best Parisian theatres, it is not
easy to rival the performance now given, and
there even the majority of the impersonations
would call for notice. The result is highly
gratifying to the public, unused to spectacles
such as are now presented to it, and is most
honourable to the management." * * * " We
may congratulate, accordingly, Mr. Hare and his
company upon a performance that lifts off a
portion of the reproach under which we have
lain, and that is the more noteworthy inasmuch

as of the dozen actors concerned in the performance, there is no one that does not deserve praise."

So great was the popularity of this production that no change of programme was needed until October, 1877, when Mr. Hare was ready with one of his most ambitious efforts.

This was the production of Lord Lytton's posthumous work "The House of Darnley," and concerning it I cannot do better than quote Mr. Dutton Cook when he said : " A critic wrote concisely of the late Lord Lytton's play of ' Not so Bad as We Seem,' that it was 'not so good as we expected.' Perhaps a like judgment might fairly be passed upon the noble author's posthumous comedy ' The House of Darnley.' It was inevitable, however, that Lord Lytton's fame should stimulate hope unduly. The author of ' The Lady of Lyons ' and ' Money ' may reasonably be reckoned the most successful dramatist " (*bien entendu* this was written in 1877) " of the nineteenth century. It may be said at once that with those established works the new comedy cannot afford comparison. But in estimating the worth of 'The House of Darnley' it is very necessary to bear in mind the peculiar conditions under which it is submitted to the public. The play was left in an unfinished state ; the whole of the last act has been furnished by Mr. Coghlan, who was without other clue than his fancy could suggest as to the original design of the dramatist. More than any other literary work, a drama must benefit by revision and reconsideration on the part of the author ; in such wise, weak points in construction may be strengthened, gaps in the story supplied, the dialogue braced, and the action quickened."

That in the face of all these very properly pointed out difficulties success should have been won speaks volumes for the tact of the courageous manager and the skill of his fellow-workers, Let me again quote my authority :

"With all its defects," he says, "'The House of Darnley' secures the attention and the respect of the audience, and succeeds in right of its own good qualities, and not merely because of the esteem in which the performances of its departed

author are generally held. If the theme be
weak, it is yet strongly handled, and demonstrates sufficiently the wit and the humour, and
the literary accomplishments of the late Lord
Lytton. The comedy has been provided for
with the good taste and liberality which have so
laudably distinguished Mr. Hare's management.
The scenes representing the oak hall at Lord
Fitzhollow's and the drawing-room and library
at Mr. Darnley's are admirable examples of the
pictorial theatre."

Acting honours in this noteworthy and praise-
worthy production were divided between Mr.
Hare (who contented himself with the small
part of Mr. Mainwaring), Mr. Kelly, Miss Ellen
Terry, and Miss Amy Roselle.

When the storm and stress of acting and
management are at an end, and Mr. Hare has
time in which to "think things over," he will no
doubt be a little bit proud of the fact that he
was responsible for the production of " The
House of Darnley."

His next venture was not very successful.
In spite of the care lavished upon its production

Mr. Tom Taylor's comedy " Victims," originally
presented at the Haymarket in 1857, failed to
attract audiences for any appreciable length of
time to the Court Theatre in 1878, and in spite
of much clever acting on the part of Mr. Hare,
who played the character of the young poet,
Mr. Herbert Fitzherbert, and his skilful company (of which his old friend and adviser,
Mr. John Clarke, was now a member), the piece
was speedily withdrawn.

Withdrawn it may unhesitatingly be said in
favour of Mr. Hare's greatest managerial success. Following his old scheme of " self effacement" he did not elect to appear in Mr. W. G.
Wills's stage version of Oliver Goldsmith's
immortal story " The Vicar of Wakefield,"
entitled " Olivia," but how far he was responsible for that beautiful production I propose to
show. It was, as a matter of fact, one of the
few plays (Mr. Hare says it was the *only* play)
in which he played the part of collaborator. He
suggested the subject to Mr. Wills, and it was
at once seized with the characteristic avidity of
that prolific and graceful writer. No one who

knew that unquestionable but erratic genius will be surprised to hear that the first draft of the play was, for stage purposes, impossible. It was made up of scenes of great beauty hopelessly choked with vast quantities of irrelevant matter. It was not consecutively written, but was jotted down at random in untidy copy-books, on the backs of used envelopes, chance scraps of paper, and even on the eager but unmethodical author's wristbands. At one time the task of bringing all this heterogeneous matter into workmanlike form seemed to be a hopeless one, but with full faith in his project and his author, Mr. Hare was not to be baffled. Night after night the two sat up together, and the play was reconstructed and rewritten in accordance with the practical managerial views. When it was at last completed Mr. Wills prudently withdrew from the scene. He had no interest in or talent for stage management, and he wisely left the production in the experienced hands of Mr. Hare, only attending the perfected rehearsal on the eve of the first performance. Mr. Hare can rarely be induced to talk about himself or about his work, but in connection with this production he is inclined to be somewhat enthusiastic. "The beauty of its subject," he says, "made the stage management of this play profoundly interesting to me, and stimulated my imagination and inventive powers to a greater height than I had ever reached. By working out the whole scheme of the play in my home study I planned out all the movements and minute stage directions, so that at the very first rehearsal it practically was the same as when it was presented to the public. The part of the Vicar I offered in the first instance to Mr. Alfred Wigan, making every effort to induce him to return to the stage in order that he might create this beautiful character. I could not induce him, however, to face the footlights again. So Mr. Hermann Vezin became the Court Vicar, and how admirably he played the part we all know."

No one grudges Mr. Vezin his splendid and well-won success, but some of us who ponder over things theatrical, sometimes wonder whether, if the Court Theatre had had another manager, and the services of Mr. John Hare

F

had been available, he might not have been induced to impersonate Dr. Primrose.

But he had his triumph in the chorus of praise with which this beautiful production was received.

"Mr. Wills," says Mr. Dutton Cook, "has been fortunate, not merely in his performers, but in his manager. Mr. Hare demonstrates anew that he has elevated theatrical decoration to the rank of a fine art; indeed, his painstaking and outlay in placing the play upon the stage justify suspicion that it was produced almost as much for its pictorial as for its dramatic merits. In either case advantage has been taken of the opportunity to present a special reflection of the artistic aspects of the last century with regard to furniture and costumes, china and glass, and other accessories. A sort of devout care has been expended upon the veriest minutiæ of upholstery and ironmongery; a fond ingenuity is apparent in every direction of the scene; and the foibles and fancies of those who love, or imagine that they love, cuckoo clocks, brass fenders, carved oak, blue-and-white crockery, and such matters, have been very liberally considered and catered for. Prettier pictures have not, indeed, been seen upon the stage than are afforded by the Primrose family, their friends and neighbours, goods and chattels, and general surroundings. But a higher claim to distinction arises from the method of its representation. In the hands of Miss Ellen Terry Olivia becomes a character of rare dramatic value. The actress's singular command of pathetic expression obtains further manifestation. The scene of Olivia's farewell to her family, all unconscious of the impending blow her flight is to inflict upon them, is curiously affecting in its subtle and subdued tenderness; while her indignation and remorse upon discovering the perfidy of Thornhill are rendered with a vehemence of emotion and tragic passion such as the modern theatre has seldom exhibited."

Of course, within the scope of this brief volume it is impossible to speak of all the actors who gained their spurs under Mr. Hare's banner, but in connection with "Olivia" it is interesting to note the success achieved at

almost the commencement of his stage career
by Mr. William Terriss as Squire Thornhill.
How " Olivia," with Sir Henry Irving as Dr.
Primrose, and Miss Ellen Terry still happily
playing the part of the sweet-souled heroine, is
to-day one of the popular items in the Lyceum
repertory, is known to all playgoers. But the
lion's share of the credit of the production
undoubtedly belongs to Mr. John Hare.

In 1879 there was a shuffling of theatrical
cards. Miss Ellen Terry migrated from the
Court to the Lyceum Theatre ; and the Kendals
returned to Mr. Hare to appear in the first
place in a revival of " A Scrap of Paper,"
supplemented by the reproduction of " A Quiet
Rubber."

A few weeks later, and at a tentative morning performance—(*matinées* were comparatively
rare events in those days)—was produced
T. W. Robertson's adaptation of the comedy
of Scribe and Legouvé, " Bataille des
Dames," entitled " The Ladies' Battle." It
is one of the works which Robertson, before
he made his mark, translated for theatrical

speculators at a price, it is said, of something like ten shillings an act. Poor Robertson! if he could only have seen his tenderly written and hitherto misunderstood work acted at the Court Theatre! To show the marked impression that was by this time being made by Mr. Hare's productions, I must again quote from the *Athenæum.* "The revival at the Court Theatre of 'The Ladies' Battle," says that authority, "has more interest and value than might be expected from the conditions under which the play was produced. For once managerial promises have been kept, and the pledge that the care that distinguishes the regular entertainments at the Court should be bestowed on the morning performances has been redeemed. How ready the public is to put faith in a management that will keep faith with it, and how much genuine interest in theatrical affairs survives the discouraging influences of recent years, is shown in the kind of audience that is assembled on such occasions as the production of a novelty at the Court. In the hands of Mr. Hare and

the one or two managers who are animated
by the same views is the future of our stage.
A performance like that of 'The Ladies'
Battle' may challenge comparison with anything that can be seen at the representative
theatres on the Continent, and the only thing
wanting to make the Court Theatre fulfil the
functions of a subventioned house is that it
should give us a certain percentage of works
of English growth, instead of an almost
constant series of adaptations." The English
plays were to follow later on, and, in the
meantime, "The Ladies' Battle," which in due
course was promoted to the evening bill,
proved a trump card. Mr. Hare's presentation of the Préfet who had changed his skin
with every Administration—had been Citizen
Montrichard under the Republic, Mons. de
Montrichard under Napoleon, and the Baron
de Montrichard under Louis XVIII.—was
one of the best performances he had ever
exhibited. In make-up and in acting it was
alike excellent. Mrs. Kendal as the heroine
acted superbly, and Mr. Kendal's powers as a

Comedian found full scope in the rather extravagantly drawn character of Gustave de Grignon. Down to every detail connected with the piece the same care was extended, and the scene in which the action passed was one of the most artistic that had ever been seen in the theatre.

It was at a morning performance, too, that Mr. G. W. Godfrey's bright and permanently popular adaptation of the French " Un Fils de Famille," happily called " The Queen's Shilling," was first given. Again the utmost care was taken with every detail, and the result was a performance which was a reflection of real life. In the character of Colonel Daunt, Mr. Hare surprised even those who had most faith in him. In the original French play, and in the English versions of it that had been seen at the Princess's and the Adelphi, the Colonel was a very formidable person, quite unlike the small but soldierlike figure that appeared at the Court. It was the boldest and, in its way, the most effective thing that Mr. Hare had done, and the impersonation, well merited the applause with which it was greeted. He was marvellously got up, and acted with extreme care and finish of style. Old playgoers will remember how Mr. and Mrs. Kendal and Mr. Hare in this pleasant play used to join in the refrain commencing " Speak to me, love, and with thy glances," and they will agree with me that they then saw comedy at its brightest and its best.

On July 19, 1879, Mr. Hare said good-bye to the Court Theatre, and in the following words, and to an enthusiastic audience, announced his forthcoming partnership with Mr. Kendal in the management of the St. James's Theatre.

" Union is strength," he said, " and I feel that in associating myself with an admirable man of business and a most able artist, and at the same time gaining the permanent services of his accomplished wife, there seems a reasonable hope of conducting successfully a theatre which up to the present time has laboured under the stigma of being unfortunate.

I assure you we shall work our hardest to reverse its ill-luck, and it will be through no lack of endeavour on our part if we fail. I may tell you that our plan of campaign will be similar to the one adopted by me here. Comedy and Comedy-drama will form the staple of our dramatic fare, and we shall endeavour to get the best company together, with a view to giving that which is always, I take it, the most satisfactory thing to an audience—an even, all-round performance."

But before opening the St. James's Theatre Mr. Hare had a new and, I think he will admit, a most delightful experience. In the company of the Kendals, and for the first time since he had become an actor of the highest note—Mr. Hare acted in the English provincial cities and towns. Always the most modest of men, he had, I have good reason to believe, a conviction that his name had never been heard of outside London, and that his methods might not suit the tastes of his country cousins. In very unmistakable terms he was soon told that his histrionic fame had travelled far and wide, and that the perfection of his art was the very thing to ensure his success among the thronged and expectant audiences that rejoiced to bid him hearty welcome. Wherever he went he at once established himself as a prime favourite, and from that day to this his provincial tours have increased in favour. No doubt London is the great and most profitable field for the English actor, but it is worth something to make one's name (as, in company with other great actors, Mr. Hare has done) a household word in all the great centres of England, Scotland and Ireland, wherever increasing industry and facilities for education naturally lead up to an increased appreciation of true art.

CHAPTER III.

THE ST. JAMES'S THEATRE.

WHEN, on October 4, 1879, the reconstructed and redecorated St. James's Theatre
was opened under the management of Messrs.
Hare and Kendal, it was freely acknowledged
to be not only one of the chief attractions but
one of the sights of London. Certainly it was
the most luxurious and tasteful playhouse that
had so far been seen in England, and the *foyer*,
which was also a picture gallery, was remarkably attractive. Indeed, the whole place
more resembled a richly appointed house than
a theatre, and there was about it a general air
that made its patrons feel themselves comfort-
ably at home.

The opening programme consisted of the

recent Court success, "The Queen's Shilling,"
with Mr. and Mrs. Kendal and Mr. Hare in
their original characters, and this was preceded
by a comedietta from the pen of Mr. Val
Prinsep (in which Mr. Hare played with
admirable art), entitled "Monsieur le Duc."

The story which this piece relates is more
familiar on the French than on the English
stage. It deals with libertinism and love.
The Duc de Richelieu, Marshal of France by
right of his military services, and *roué* by reason
of his numerous profligacies, receives a visit
from a young lady—an orphan—who, obeying
the injunctions of a dying mother, seeks his
powerful protection. After his wont, the Duke
bets lightly on the immediate dishonour of his
fair visitor, professing to regard her appeal as
nothing but a direct venture of her innocence.
The bet is lost. In the subject of his gallantry
he discovers his own daughter, her mother (a
lady of noble rank, but not his equal in point of
birth) having married the Duke when a young
man, for which indiscretion a *lettre de cachet*,
procured at the instance of his father, had

consigned Monsieur le Duc to temporary seclusion in the Bastille. Meanwhile the mother had been spirited away. Richelieu having still a lingering affection for the wife of his younger days, and reflecting on the past with its rudely checked happiness, receives his daughter to his arms. The heartless libertine becomes the repentant father whose one thought is to protect his child from insult and wrong.

This cleverly conceived and well-written little play has not been revived, but it is mentioned at some length in these pages, because in it Mr. Hare at the commencement of his new partnership struck out a new line and made a perfect picture of Monsieur le Duc.

On December 18 of the same year the St. James's management did itself honour in producing " The Falcon," an original play in one act, by Alfred Tennyson, founded on the story in " The Decameron " of Boccaccio. This interesting piece was beautifully staged, and as the Count Alberighi and the Lady Giovanna Mr. and Mrs. Kendal played perfectly. The trouble of the cast was the falcon, who died during the run of the play.

The next venture on the part of the new management was the highly popular revival of Tom Taylor's well-known play, "Still Waters Run Deep." In this Mrs. Kendal made a very notable hit as Mrs. Sternhold, Mr. Kendal was admirable as John Mildmay, and in the comparatively small part of Potter Mr. Hare excelled himself. It was a masterpiece of character-acting, faultless in get-up and, indeed, in all respects. As one of the most eminent critics summed it up, it was in very truth "a keen instance of unexaggerated eccentricity."

In connection with "Still Waters Run Deep," Mr. Hare has one of those stories to tell that prove how presence of mind exercised in the right way and at the right moment may avert serious calamity. With Mr. and Mrs. Kendal and the St. James's Theatre company he was, while on one of those provincial tours that had now become their annual custom, playing the piece at the Prince of Wales's Theatre, Liverpool. The occasion was the Kendals' benefit, and as a matter of course the house was packed from floor to ceiling. In those days precautions against fire and panic were not so rigidly enforced as they are now, and to make room for the overwhelming audience the orchestra had been banished to the regions below the stage, and all the gangways were blocked with chairs. Under these conditions anything like a scare would inevitably have been attended by horrible consequences. Now those who are familiar with "Still Waters Run Deep" will remember that when the curtain rises on the first act all the principal characters are discovered. John Mildmay, Mrs. Mildmay, and Mrs. Sternhold are in the front of the stage, and old Potter is seated at the back napping by the fireside, with his back to the audience and a handkerchief thrown over his head and face. On the evening of which I am writing, the fire in the grate, or the lamp which was supposed to represent the fire, had been lit, and as good luck had it there was a hole in old Potter's handkerchief. Through this Mr. Hare, impersonating that eccentric old gentleman, saw, to his intense horror, that the flames had caught that part of the scene painted to represent the mantelpiece, and were slowly but surely creeping up and gaining ground. As the scene of his earliest appearances he knew the theatre well, and had often recognised the fact (it is all altered now) that in the case of an alarm it would with a full house prove a veritable death-trap. He also knew that if the crowded audience saw the steadily increasing flames, a panic with its ghastly results would ensue. Fortunately some moments had to elapse before he was called upon to take his cue, and slowly rising and in the slip-shod manner he assumed in portraying the character, toddled off the stage. His exit caused considerable laughter, and Mrs. Kendal, turning to see the cause of the unexpected interruption, realised with characteristic quickness the perilous predicament. Instantly grasping the situation, and the reason of Mr. Hare's departure, she placed herself, with admirable calmness, between the ignited scenery and the audience. Meantime Mr. Hare was behind the scenes. "The

Fireman!" he called, but there was no fireman. "The Gasman then!" he demanded, but the gasman "had just stepped out to smoke his pipe." Such was the manner in which in those days some of the provincial theatres were conducted! Happily he obtained a wet blanket, and this, with the assistance of a carpenter, was pushed through the fireplace from the back to the front of the scene, and wrapped round the flame, which, not without considerable difficulty was extinguished. The bare arms of the workman, the blanket, and the fire were all this time hidden from the audience by Mrs. Kendal. The danger being over, Mr. Hare returned to the stage with the same comic walk, and Mrs. Kendal interpolated a "Well, brother Potter, and where have *you* been?" She laughed, and so did the audience, little knowing that through the courage and presence of mind of their entertainers they had escaped a terrible catastrophe.

Encouraged by the popularity of the revived "Still Waters Run Deep"—and in the dearth of any brilliant novelty from the pen of a living dramatist—the St. James's management, after the reproduction of " The Ladies' Battle," set to work on another old and well-tried play, the delightful " Black-Eyed Susan " of Douglas Jerrold. As the hero and heroine of this breezy and stirring drama, the Kendals had already made their mark, but in order to suit the tastes of fashionable West-end audiences the play was partly rewritten and in many ways altered by Mr. W. G. Wills. Not a few play-goers who loved the old play as it stood, and some critics who not unnaturally shared their feelings, were inclined to take umbrage at this, but the managers were right. To have given the original " Black-Eyed Susan " to a St. James's audience in 1880 would have been a mistake. It would have been misunderstood, and would probably have been received with laughter instead of sympathy. As it was, the piece was beautifully handled both by play-wright and by players, and its fault was its overwhelming pathos. Who, who heard it, will ever forget Mrs. Kendal's prayer in the last supremely rendered scene!

Once more the stage management caused surprise as well as delight. " To see," wrote a keen critic, " such pictures as those of the cottage at Deal, in which the action of ' William and Susan ' commences, the beach with the fleet in the Downs, the cabin of the man-of-war with the officers with their smooth-shaven faces, and in their knee-breeches and silk stockings, and the marines with their quaint but effective costume of the early part of this century, and the final tableau of the deck of the same vessel, in which everything is exact enough to defy scrutiny, is to learn of what the art of theatrical decoration is capable. The improvement, meanwhile, is not confined to matters of dress and to what is inanimate in the picture. For the first time upon an English stage, supers of whom everyone apparently is an actor are employed. The pictures afforded accordingly vibrate with life, and the stage illusion is perfect. So thoroughly has Mr. Hare accomplished the task he set himself that his example must inevitably be followed, and a definite improvement in the conditions of theatrical representation in England is now a mere matter of time."

This was written fifteen years ago, and we all know how perfectly things are done in the best theatres of to-day. That much of this perfection is due to the example set by Mr. Hare, and (I know that in speaking of the St. James's productions he would like to add) Mr. Kendal,—is beyond all dispute.

In " William and Susan " Mr. Hare appeared (what a lesson to the much discussed actor-manager !) in the trivial part of the Admiral, and to the immense good of the production supplied a picture accurate and faithful in all respects.

Octave Feuillet's well-known story " Le Roman d'un Jeune Homme Pauvre " has always had a fascination for English playwrights and actors. In 1859, a stage version of it was produced under the title of " Ivy Hall," at the Princess's, and though the play is long since forgotten, the production will always have an interesting place in theatrical lore, inasmuch as in one of its minor characters Sir Henry Irving made his first appearance on the London stage.

Eight years later, Dr. Westland Marston prepared another adaptation of the novel for the late E. A. Sothern, which was produced at the Haymarket in 1868 under the title of "A Hero of Romance." In this, as old playgoers will remember, Sothern, who always loved to do startling things, made a tremendous sensation by an alarming jump that he took from the summit of a ruined tower into the unseen depths below the stage. In connection with Sothern's famous leap, I recall a droll incident. He was playing the piece in a provincial town, he had met with a slight accident, and made up his mind that for a few nights it would be wiser to jump by proxy. Accordingly he engaged a professional acrobat of his own height and build, who dressed exactly like him, and who (hidden of course from the audience) was stationed at the top of the tower ready to take his leaping cue from Sothern as he made his frenzied rush up the dilapidated stairs. Now Sothern, as most of us know, had a mania for practical joking, and it generally happened that amongst his company were victims of his propensity longing for an opportunity to pay him back in his own coin. This chance seemed to come to the company in question when the acrobat spoke rather sneeringly of the jump, and said that if he could only have a spring board he could "shoot right up into the flies and turn a double somersault before he came down; but he supposed Mr. Sothern wouldn't like it." The actors assured him that nothing would please Sothern better, and so the spring board was provided, and the plot perfected.

"Victor! 't is death!" cried the heroine, on the stage, when Sothern stated his apparently mad determination to leap from the crazy battlements.

"Death!" answered Sothern, in his most impressive tone, "'Tis honour!"—and dashed up the stairs to give the cue to his confederate and crouch behind the scenery. "W–s–s–h–h!" like a rocket the actor seemed to spring sky-wards, and then, turning an exquisite double somersault, disappeared from view. The good people of the provincial town of which I am writing took it all seriously,—marvelled at Sothern's proficiency—and in acknowledgment of his prowess called him any number of times before the curtain. It was some time before he discovered the cause of this extraordinary enthusiasm, and when he did there was—in addition to a dismissed acrobat—trouble in that company.

Probably it was the memory of Sothern's undoubted success as this "Hero of Romance" that induced the St. James's management to commission Mr. Coghlan to turn to the pages of "Le Roman d'un Jeune Homme Pauvre;" but when "Good Fortune," as the piece was now called, was produced it was found that the once sparkling wine had become flat and lost its flavour. Why is it that plays that at one time seemed so fascinating grow (it is a term that those who write about the stage are, in default of a better one, apt to use) "old-fashioned"? To those who have loved and been impressed by them in the days of long ago the word can never apply. I suppose the truth of the matter is that the fare that seems perfectly satisfactory to one generation of playgoers does not suit the more fastidious palates of those who succeed them.   Be that as it may, " Good Fortune," although Mr. Coghlan had done his work admirably, and Mr. and Mrs. Kendal and their supporters (Mr. Hare had no part in the piece) played to perfection, did not prove too attractive at the St. James's ; and I don't believe it would have done even if (with or without the aid of an acrobat) Mr. Kendal had courted favour (which he very wisely did not) in Sothern's sensational leap.

But the comparative failure of " Good Fortune " had a curious effect not only on the St. James's Theatre but upon the English stage. Sooner or later the admirable work of Mr. A. W. Pinero would have been certain to find its home, and make its mark, but he would probably own that his first great chance came when Mr. Hare and Mr. Kendal suddenly found themselves in want of an attraction, and determined to produce " The Money Spinner," a two-act play that had made note in the provinces.   It was the old story of the right time coming for the right man.   In the days of 1881 we sadly wanted a new dramatist. Mr. Pinero suddenly filled the gap, and in spite of the brilliant and successful playwrights who have, with infinite credit to themselves and incalculable advantage to the stage, followed his lead, he still holds his own as the *premier* dramatist of to-day.

No doubt Mr. Pinero would be the first to admit that his first London chance with an important play was an extraordinary one With such artists as Mr. John Hare, Mr. and Mrs. Kendal, Mr. John Clayton, Mr. Mackintosh, and Miss Kate Phillips in his leading parts, he had indeed little left to wish for ; but the play succeeded as well as those who acted in it, and how splendidly he has followed up the promise of his first fruits is known to everyone.

Mr. Hare's part was that of the self-styled Baron Croodle, and some critics consider that his rendering of the character of that disreputable old Chevalier d'Industrie, a Montague Tigg and a Chevy Slyme rolled into one—was so far first and foremost in his gallery of character studies. His make-up and disguise as the drink-sodden and card-swindling old reprobate, with his shabby clothes showing clearly the evidence of more affluent days, and his still swaggering and half-patronising manner, were alike remarkable. Every little detail of the character had been minutely studied, every little item of make-up and costume carefully thought out. I have seen representatives of Baron Croodle who, with no little success, only gave the comic side of a wonderfully drawn character. When Mr. Hare played the part he made it not only humorous but in its peculiar way pathetic. When he surreptitiously lifted his brandy flask to his lips, or when he in a half-lordly fashion asked the naturally high-minded daughter he had trained to cheat if " there was any little dispute at cards that dear papa could settle," we laughed at, but we pitied him. It was a truthfully limned picture of a man capable of better things who had wilfully allowed himself to go down hill and had dragged his women-folk with him. The impersonation possessed the whimsical pathos of Newman Noggs, and the irresistible but transparent bluster of Captain

Costigan, and was in its way unique. Mr. Hare has before now been called the Meissonier of the stage. He never had a greater claim to that title than when he conceived, drew, and carefully "stippled in" the portrait of Mr. Pinero's Baron Croodle. If in the days of long ago Mr. Hare had not made his lasting reputation, this inimitable impersonation would have at once and for always established it. Never shall I forget how after the run of the play in London it was received and relished in the provinces. Indeed, Mr. Hare's Baron Croodle, Mrs. Kendal's Millicent, and Mr. Kendal's Lord Kengussie are among the most cherished of theatrical recollections.

And yet, in spite of its popularity, the story of "The Money Spinner" was rather a painful one, and a good many people were inclined to agree with "Mr. Punch" when he said : "And now comes the wonder, namely, that an author should have chosen such materials for a piece, have managed them so skilfully, and have had the luck to get it so perfectly played as to cause its objectionable character and its wrong moral to be lost sight of in the real interest awakened by the personages in the short drama."

The characters of Claude Melnotte and Pauline Deschappelles have always been favourite ones with Mr. and Mrs. Kendal, and April, 1881, witnessed the very welcome revival of "The Lady of Lyons." In this Mr. Hare appeared as Colonel Damas, and was excellent in all respects. Great care had been taken with the *mise en scène*, which was adequate and unobtrusive.

For the difficult task of adapting "Le Fils de Coralie" of Mons. Albert Delpit, for the English stage, the services of Mr. G. W. Godfrey, who had done such excellent work for the management in "The Queen's Shilling," were retained. "'Le Fils de Coralie,'" said a critic, "is a powerful and, strange to say, sympathetic play. Just so far as it adheres to the original, the English version may claim the same praise. Each step from the beaten track, however, takes it into the mud, and when, in the last act, the path is quitted, piece and acting both disappear in a quagmire."

But in spite of the disagreeable materials of which it was composed, "Coralie," as the play was now called, was so well acted by all concerned in it, and so perfectly staged, that it proved attractive. As the heroine, Mrs. Kendal obtained a triumph. A display of passion more powerful or more varied than was exhibited in the second and third acts, in which the lost woman saw the spectres of her past life rise up in judgment against her, and chase her from the home and happiness she fondly imagined herself to have won, the English stage had seldom seen. Its influence over the audience was overpowering. Mr. Hare's Mr. Critchell,—the keenest of keen lawyers—was a piece of absolute interpretation.

In November, T. W. Robertson's adaptation of "L'Aventurière" of Mons. Emile Augier, which, with Sothern in the leading part, was produced at the Haymarket in 1869, was staged. This reproduction of the still familiar "Home" was very acceptable. Mr. Kendal followed Sothern as Colonel White ; Mrs. Kendal (playing with unimpeachable taste and pathos)

succeeded Miss Ada Cavendish in her fine
impersonation of Mrs. Pinchbeck, and the dead
author's son, the younger T. W. Robertson
(alas! he, too, has gone over to the great
majority!) was, in the character of the boy,
Bertie Thompson, made welcome on the
London stage.   Mr. Hare elected to appear as
the rascally and dissolute Captain Mountraffe,
the part that at the Haymarket had been so
splendidly acted by Mr. Compton.   He played
the character with such merciless fidelity as to
make the creature exactly what he was—
absolutely odious.   Some censors declared that
both in appearance and manner he was so
abject, that his presence in a country house was
inconceivable ; but if that was so it was the
fault of the author, not of the actor.   When
Mr. Hare takes a part it is a truthful photo-
graph of the man he has in his mind's eye ; not
a feeble portrait touched up to suit a sitter and
his friends.   His Captain Mountraffe was not a
pleasant picture, but its memory will live with
all who saw it.

In conjunction with " Home " was produced

Mr. Clement Scott's delightful one-act play founded on the "Jeanne qui Pleure, et Jeanne qui Rit," of MM. Dumanoir and De Kéranion, called "The Cape Mail," in which Mrs. Kendal acted with inimitable art.

The end of this eventful year was reserved for its greatest triumph. Mr. Pinero's "The Money Spinner" had paved the way for "The Squire," which, to a distinguished and delighted audience, was performed for the first time on December 29. Here at last was what we had been longing and waiting for : a successful home-made play worthy to rank with the best efforts of our leading dramatists. In every way the work was welcome, and truly it was said that, "The fresh, breezy atmosphere of 'The Squire' carries us away from the busy world and takes us into scenes of charming rural life. The play is redolent of country air and pure domestic scenes that are a relief from the every-day incidents of a town life, and as hearty and welcome as they are fresh and singularly pleasing."

Of this pre-eminently satisfactory production

Mr. Clement Scott wrote : " Mr. Pinero has given us persons, not sketches; his characters are flesh and blood, and his dialogue is, from first to last, admirable, and the very thing that the stage requires. Mr. Mackintosh has created old Gunnion. It is an embodiment, a personation, of an abstract idea. He makes the man live before us, and it is emphatically the finest bit of character acting that has been seen on the stage for many years. Almost as good, in its way, is the grumpy old parson played by Mr. Hare, a character not sufficiently praised for subtlety and finish, the last in the long gallery of character portraits painted by this accomplished actor. Mrs. Kendal has no living rival in strong emotional characters. She holds her audiences and quickly touches their sympathies. Her 'Squire,' however, is a part of exceptional difficulty, requiring all the finesse of the finished actress. The one great difficulty Mrs. Kendal got over with a taste, a discretion, and a nature that have not deserted her for an instant since she startled her admirers with ' The Ladies' Battle.' In Mr. Kendal she has a loyal assistant, and it is sometimes the misfortune of such loyalty to be compelled to play parts necessarily of the same pattern and without much variety. All plays must have love, and, consequently, lovers. Mr. Kendal seems to possess the gift of eternal youth, and so he must go on making love for ever. Mr. Frederic Clay has written some charming music to help one of the village scenes, and it is altogether a stage treat that no one should miss."

Of the manner in which it was produced and performed, the *Athenæum* said : " Long bent upon imparting to English representations the vitality, finish, and *ensemble* which characterized the performance of the Dutch comedians recently in England, Mr. Hare has at length succeeded in his task. From highest to lowest every part in the piece was well played and the spectacle perfect. Its merits were not confined to the excellence of the collective representation. Separate performances were admirable. Like most of her recent presentations, Mrs. Kendal's Kate Verity was unsurpassable in truth and power, and reached a point of inten-

H

sity which riveted the audience. Mr. Hare assigned a distinct and striking individuality to the part of the clergyman, and Mr. Kendal played Lieutenant Thorndyke with much earnestness and some passion. Mr. Wenman's Gilbert Hythe was a fine and masculine piece of acting, which could not easily have been better. Two specimens of bucolic life were played by Messrs. Mackintosh and Brandon in remarkable style. The Gunnion of Mr. Mackintosh may claim, indeed, to be one of the most noteworthy performances in its class that our stage has seen. Mr. T. W. Robertson gave a capital sketch of a gipsy boy. 'The Squire' was a complete success, and its reception was enthusiastic."

Mr. Brandon, it may be noted, has developed into the popular actor-author of to-day—Mr. Brandon Thomas.

When "The Squire" was brought into the country, Mr. Hare played old Gunnion with such exquisite humour and perfect finish that many people wondered why he had not elected to appear in the character on the first production of the play. But when the piece was revived in London he generously allowed Mr. Mackintosh to go on scoring in the part, and returned to his original character of the Mad Parson. So great was the success of "The Squire," that no novelty was wanted at the St. James's until December, 1882, when Mr. B. C. Stephenson's clever adaptation of MM. Xavier de Montépin and Kervani's "La Maison du Mari" entitled "Impulse" was produced. Unluckily there was in this no part for Mr. Hare, but it was in every way a brilliantly successful production, and still remains a most popular item in the repertory of Mr. and Mrs. Kendal.

In October, 1883, Mr. Hare made his reappearance, playing for the first time the exacting character of old Rogers in "Young Folks' Ways," a comedy in five acts by Mrs. Burnett and Mr. W. H. Gillette, founded on Mrs. Burnett's story of "Esmeralda." Mr. Hare had never presented a finer or more telling picture. The meek, peace loving old man, whose surrender to his truculent wife amounts to his absolute effacement, but whom love for his daughter rouses at length into sturdy self-assertion, was presented with noble skill. At first it was thought that in old Rogers the actor had secured a character after his own heart. He introduced the old man admirably, with many delicate touches, all his artistic instinct, and an undercurrent of sly humour. But the character died out of the story, and its impersonator could not supply an interest that after a time ceased to exist. Mrs. Kendal played so bewitchingly as Nora Desmond, and was so well supported by Mr. Kendal, whose light comedy style is always admirable, that the scenes between them were irresistible. Mr. George Alexander, who was now a member of the company at the St. James's,—the theatre that he manages to-day, with honour to himself and advantage to dramatic art—was the Dave Hardy of the cast.

In December "A Scrap of Paper" was revived, and in this, as I have foreshadowed, Mr. Hare forsook the small part of Archie Hamilton, to which he formerly gave importance, and appeared as Dr. Penguin, F.Z.S.

April 17, 1884, was the birthday of another St. James's triumph: Mr. A. W. Pinero's English version of Mons. Georges Ohnet's "Le Maître de Forges," entitled "The Ironmaster." It was immediately successful, and in the hands of the Kendals has borne the test of repeated revival. It was one of their trump cards in America, and at the time that I am writing— eleven years since its first production—they are playing it to crowded and enthusiastic audiences in the principal English provincial towns.

In the original cast Mr. Hare took no part, but later, in the country, he showed by his delightfully humorous rendering of the character of old Moulinet, the manufacturer of chocolates, that it contained a part with which, comparatively small though it was, he could do great things.

It was hardly likely that a company such as the St. James's in these days would be content without the revival of one of Shakespeare's comedies. As Orlando and Rosalind Mr. and Mrs. Kendal had already worthily won their laurels; and accordingly on January 24, 1885,

" As You Like It " was staged with a scenic perfection that had never before been seen. But
the patrons of the house were not accustomed,
and apparently did not much care to see their
favourites in Shakespeare, and not a few of
them were ungracious enough to declare that in
their generous efforts to give a beautiful production the management had been too lavish. Mr.
Lewis Wingfield, who was responsible for the
adornment of the play, laid the action in the
time of Charles VII. of France, and dressed it
accordingly. The costumes were historically
correct, rich in material, and exquisite in design,
while the scenery was as realistic and beautiful
as money and theatrical art could make it. It
was all very much admired, but it was the
correct thing at the time to say that it was
" too modern " and " rather overdone." Mr.
Hare appeared as Touchstone, and was much
praised for the manner in which he merged his
own individuality in the nature of the philoso-
phizing clown.

In the following month, Mr. Hare took the
chair at the annual dinner of the Dramatic and

Musical Sick Fund, and in the course of an eloquent and convincing address, said : " It was with the greatest diffidence that I accepted the position that I now most unworthily fill, but I was, in spite of many objections and protestations on my part, over persuaded by the committee who have so honoured me by asking me to be your chairman on this most interesting occasion. Therefore, without wishing to repay the compliment they have paid me by an ungracious retort, I must warn them that their sins are upon their own heads, and that for mine, both of omission and commission, they must be responsible. Seriously, to occupy a chair from which, in the past, the eloquence of giants like Dickens, Thackeray, Benjamin Webster, and others has been employed in the interests of this charity, makes one feel a veritable pigmy, and overwhelms me with confusion. To quote the words that Shakespeare puts into the mouth of his clown, Touchstone, ' A man, if he was of a fearful heart, might well nigh stagger in this attempt.' Gentlemen, I am a man of a fearful heart, and I do stagger in the attempt; I feel myself a kind of oratorical Blondin who, with balancing pole in hand, amidst the gaze of eager onlookers, essays to cross the rapids; but I have more than myself to consider in the difficult passage that I am about to take, for on my back I carry a child for whose safety I am responsible—that child the well deserving charity whose cause I am here to plead to-night." After urging this cause with distinct and substantial effect, Mr. Hare said: "Perhaps I may be forgiven if, before I finish, I tell you a little story which has a certain bearing on my appeal to you to-night. It was told me by a friend who was staying in a country house where a large number of people were assembled. On a certain occasion the bishop of the diocese was to preach a charity sermon. The majority of the guests of course attended the service, one amongst them being one of the richest men in England. My friend, who is a man not very well to do in the world, sat next to the old gentleman in church, and fully expecting at least a five-pound note to be put into the plate by the millionaire, made ready his sovereign, but when the plate came round beheld the very rich man put in a shilling, and my friend, frankly admitting that his astonishment was tempered with relief, changed his coin, and also put in a shilling. Let me implore you not to follow this example—let those who intend to give little give much ; let those who intend to give much give more. Gentlemen, I have nearly staggered across those rapids I spoke of, and am nearing the opposite shore—how far successfully my journey has been accomplished I cannot say, for I dare not look behind me. You, who have watched my faltering steps, must be indulgent to one who appears to-night in a new and unaccustomed *rôle.* It only remains for me now to make a final appeal to you on behalf of the suffering and distressed, to ask those who are successful and fortunate amongst you to remember those that are fallen by the way in life's journey ; to ask you to loosen your heart strings and your purse strings on behalf of the poor and destitute. The actor's calling has two sides : the one bright,

exciting, and, to the world, much that is fascinating ; but the reverse of the picture is a sad
one : disappointed hopes, unsuccessful struggles,
too often ending in misery and despair.   It is
for those unfortunates that I plead, and I ask
all those to whom Fortune has been kind to
give willing, cheerful, and generous help,
bearing in mind the words of the inspired
writer, that when the sum of all earthly virtues
is arrived at,—' The greatest of all is charity.' "

Other notable speeches on this occasion were
made by Mr. J. Comyns Carr, Mr. W. S.
Gilbert, Mr. Hermann Vezin, Mr. Marcus
Stone, Mr. Val Prinsep, and Mr. S. B. Bancroft.
It was then indeed that Mr. Gilbert introduced
his " famous young lady of fifteen," who sits in
the middle of the front row of the dress circle
" on the rare occasion of the first performance
of an original English play."

" She is a very charming girl," said Mr.
Gilbert, " gentle, modest, sensitive, carefully
educated and delicately nurtured, very easily
flurried and perhaps a little too apt to take
alarm when no occasion for alarm exists, but,

nevertheless, an excellent specimen of a well, bred young English gentlewoman ; and it is with reference to its suitability to the eyes and the ears of this young lady that the moral fitness of every original English play is gauged on the occasion of its production. It must contain no allusions that cannot be fully and satisfactorily explained to this young lady ; it must contain no incident, no dialogue that can by any chance summon a blush to this young lady's innocent face."

Of course, Mr. Gilbert's young lady of fifteen exists to-day, but I think he would admit that she has within recent years had facilities for learning a good deal, and that in 1895 her parents, or guardians, are not quite so sensitive on her behalf as they were ten years ago.

The next novelty at the St. James's was " Mayfair," being Mr. Pinero's adaptation of Mons. Victorien Sardou's " La Maison Neuve." Although this much discussed and powerful play had been produced at the Vaudeville Theatre, Paris, as long ago as 1866, it was so essentially French in tone and treatment that no English playwright had so far ventured to lay hands on it.   Mr. Pinero accomplished his difficult task with infinite skill and discretion, but even he, backed up by the splendid cast that interpreted his work, could not make the play permanently popular in London.   It contained fine acting parts for Mr. and Mrs. Kendal, but with all the art at their command they could not make them sympathetic, and the most popular personage in the play was Nicholas Barrable, the warm-hearted old stock-broker.   In the hands of Mr. Hare this was a delightful impersonation.   It was a picture that might have stepped from the pages of Dickens or Thackeray.   The shrewd, sound and cordial old fellow made many friends while he appeared at the St. James's, and the impersonation set many critics wondering why Mr. Hare did not venture on Got's famous part in " Le Gendre de Mons. Poirier."   " Mayfair," which was produced on October 31, 1885, was, of course, perfectly staged.   The scene that represented Barrable's home in Bloomsbury was the essence of unobtrusive but **effective stage art.**

"Mayfair" was succeeded by a revival of "Impulse," and on February 13, 1886, a brilliant audience extended a hearty welcome to "Antoinette Rigaud," a three-act play adapted from the French of "Mons. Raymond Deslandes" by Mr. Ernest Warren. Mr. and Mrs. Kendal were this time provided with thoroughly congenial parts which they played to perfection, and as General de Préfond, Mr. Hare gave another of his masterly character sketches. In this clever, dramatic, well-constructed, interesting and perfectly-acted play there was a touching scene between Mrs. Kendal and Mr. Hare that, exquisitely acted as it was, will never be forgotten.

"Antoinette Rigaud" was succeeded on May 25, by Messrs. Sydney Grundy and Sutherland Edwards's adaptation in five acts of the "Martyre" of MM. D'Ennery and Tarbé, entitled "The Wife's Sacrifice." The English playwrights had done their work well. Mr. and Mrs. Kendal (the latter especially) were provided with telling characters, and Mr. Hare found an attractive though not very great part in Mr. Drake, an English Consul from Pondicherry, who is always protesting that he minds no one's business but his own, and, as a matter of consequence, is always mixed up in other people's affairs. Mr. Hare's appearance as this neat and dapper little English gentleman, with his dry and sententious manner (but thoroughly warm heart), in the midst of foreign surroundings, was a great relief to a somewhat gloomy play, and formed one of its conspicuous successes. On the fall of the curtain on the first night of the performance of the play, and after loud calls for all the principal characters, the authors, and the adapters, Mr. Hare made a brief and interesting speech, in which he said that Mons. D'Ennery had intended to be present to see the play performed for the first time in its English dress, but was prevented from doing so by illness. Mr. Hare also rightly urged the value of applause to the actors, though he discreetly added that by applause it was not always possible to gauge the success of a play.

To my mind, Mr. Hare has rarely been seen to greater advantage than in Mr. Pinero's clever

three-act comedy, " The Hobby Horse," produced at the St James's on October 23, 1886.
As Mr. Spencer Jermyn, the cheery, spruce,
and precise " patron of the turf," the dramatist
had taken his measure to a nicety, and fitted
him like the proverbial and much quoted glove.
No better stage-portrait has ever been limned
than this alternately urbane and peppery little
gentleman, so happily nick-named " Nettles " by
his affectionate but much perplexed wife. For
a good many playgoers " The Hobby Horse,"
with its quaint and subtle humour, was a little
bit before its time. When, with Mr. Hare in
his original character of Spencer Jermyn, it is—
as it assuredly must be—revived, it will, if I
mistake not, make a great mark. Mr. Hare
should be prevailed upon to play this splendidly
drawn character during his forthcoming tour
in America. His impersonation of Spencer
Jermyn is undoubtedly worthy to rank with
his Lord Ptarmigant, Prince Perovsky, Sam
Gerridge, Beau Farintosh, Lord Kilclare, Baron
Croodle, and Benjamin Goldfinch, and higher
praise than this cannot be given it.

It was the last original character that he was to play during his partnership with Mr. Kendal at the St. James's Theatre. In the revival of "Lady Clancarty" (Tom Taylor's play had been originally produced at the Olympic Theatre in 1874), which took place on March 3, 1887, he did not appear. That his friends and admirers had hoped that he would undertake the part of William III. (this would no doubt have been an exquisite impersonation) was patent to him was evinced in the little speech before the curtain that, in response to incessant calls, he was compelled to make. The excuse, he said, for not appearing as the king was the brilliant success made in that part by Mr. Mackintosh. This was no doubt graceful, and as far as Mr. Mackintosh was concerned, it was perfectly true, but we should all have liked to see Mr. Hare as "Dutch William." The piece was as perfectly mounted as it was splendidly acted by Mr. and Mrs. Kendal, and the other members of this famous company. To ensure the accuracy of the costumes of the period, the management had secured the assistance of Mr.

Marcus Stone, and exact reproductions were given of old tapestries, mantelpieces, furniture, and other appointments. As a critic pointed out: " In this age of careful and expensive productions there has been none more beautiful more accurate and splendid than ' Lady Clancarty ' at the St. James's Theatre ; no detail, however trifling, has been neglected, All is beautiful and grateful to the senses, and if the play should fail to enthral or touch the mind there is a feast of stage pictures that cannot fail to give complete and utter satisfaction to the eye."

" Lady Clancarty " had a long and successful run, and after a series of acceptable revivals, the partnership of Messrs. Hare and Kendal came to an end. On July 21, 1888, " The Squire " was played to a crowded, enthusiastic, and sympathetic audience, and when the curtain fell, Mr. Hare stepped before it and said :

" Ladies and Gentlemen, I had hoped that in your kindness you might have spared me making a speech on this, to me, most trying occasion, but your cordial demonstration leaves

me no loophole to escape from addressing a
few remarks to you on this the last night of my
joint management of the St. James's Theatre.
I speak for myself now alone, and I am sure
my friend Mr. Kendal will follow me, and
express his own feelings on the subject.   It has
often occurred to me that it must be a most
painful thing for an author to write the word
'Finis' at the end of a work which has cost
much loving thought and toil.   I myself as a
reader have often felt deep regret at coming to
the end of that which has stimulated my
imagination and aroused my sympathies and
touched my sense of humour.   I can safely say
that, as a manager, to close this important
chapter of my theatrical life is to me a source of
both sorrow and regret ; and although it would
be a presumption in me to hope that you as
readers have been influenced by such feelings as
I have described, I still may flatter myself that
in recalling the record of the past nine years of
management that I have shared with my friend
Mr. Kendal, there may be some bright spots
that your memories may linger upon with satis-

faction and approval. Be that as it may, we have done our best. We have done our best inasmuch as, whilst fighting to live amidst a keen and vigorous competition, we have endeavoured not to forget the advancement of our art in the more sordid care of theatrical management. It has been argued to our prejudice that we have favoured too much the productions of foreign authors; but I would ask you to remember that in the matter of plays, the demand has ever been greater than the supply, and that the history of the English stage for many years has proved it to be incapable of being entirely independent of foreign work; and surely it would be as unjust, ungenerous, and narrow-minded to endeavour to limit the attention of English audiences to works of their own playwrights, as it would be to forbid the sale of works of fiction and fact that have originated in the brains of distinguished foreigners. I can safely say, however, that to England we have always turned first for the dramatic fare that we have placed before you, and although our resources have been narrowed from the fact

that our school and our method is essentially a
modern one, we have been able to present to
you many English comedies, and have had the
privilege of introducing to you in his more
serious aspect one of the most distinguished of
our modern playwrights, Mr. Arthur W. Pinero.
That we have not done more has been our
misfortune; I would like to think not altogether
our fault. Be that as it may, we owe a deep
debt of gratitude to you, our public, for the
support and encouragement you have given us
when we have deserved it; your consideration
and indulgence when we have failed to satisfy
the demands you made upon us. For both I
thank you. I must also publicly thank the
partner whose loyal aid and help I have
enjoyed for so many years, Mrs. Kendal, whose
talents have shed lustre upon and given vitality
to so many of our productions; also a company,
many of whom I am proud to count as friends
of old standing, and a devoted staff of officials
and servants, for being in a position at
this present of hoping I may enjoy some portion of your confidence and regard in the future."

Following this, Mr. Kendal said :

" It is perhaps somewhat singular that the first time I should have to speak from these footlights words not set down for me by my author, should be in taking farewell of you and the St. James's Theatre under its present management. For Mrs. Kendal and myself I most cordially and gratefully endorse all that my friend, Mr. Hare, has just said in acknowledgment of the great indulgence and the most generous support which we have received at your hands during our tenancy of this theatre. We have had more successes and fewer failures than fall to the lot of average managers. It would be an affectation on my part, were I to be restrained by any unworthy bashfulness from declaring that for our successes we are principally indebted to Mrs. Kendal. With Mrs. Kendal we have done what we have done; without her, we could, indeed, have done but little. No one, I am sure, will more sincerely endorse this avowal than my late partner, to whose uninterrupted friendship, hearty loyalty, and generous co-operation during our entire connection, I now most gladly bear testimony. Next to Mrs. Kendal, we are indebted to the zealous assistance and unsparing efforts of our entire company and staff, who, without exception, have done their utmost in aiding us to earn the commendation so liberally accorded by our critics, to whom we gratefully admit our obligations. One of the kindest and yet keenest of our critics has said, that the partnership now terminated has been productive of much interesting and memorable work. If we have done this, I may frankly say we have realised our highest ambition. In closing a connection of such long duration, and parting from our company, out partner, and the theatre which has been so many years our home, we have but words of heartfelt gratitude for the past, and confident hope for the future. And now, ladies and gentlemen, the time has come to say, in this place, Farewell. We separate from our recent associations with no inconsiderable pain. Ties such as we have maintained with the St. James's Theatre through all these years are not broken without regret. We go each our way, with no shadow of rivalry save the worthy rivalry of striving each for himself and herself to earn a continuance of your favour, and to sustain the honour of our profession."

Mr. Hare was right. Even after this lapse of years, it is a painful thing to write " Finis " to that memorable chapter of English dramatic history that records the Hare and Kendal management of the St. James's Theatre. What was done in the production of plays these pages have briefly retold, but before ending it will be pleasant as well as instructive to note some of the well-known names of those who took part in them. From time to time the company included Mrs. Gaston Murray, Miss Kate Phillips, Miss Cissy Grahame, Miss Linda Dietz, Mrs. Stephens, Miss Kate Pattison, Miss Louise Moodie, Miss Winifred Emery, Miss Kate Bishop, Miss M. Cathcart, Miss Ada Murray, Mrs. Hermann Vezin, Miss Webster, Miss May Whitty, Miss Vane, Miss Lydia Cowell, Miss Fanny Enson, Mrs. Beerbohm Tree (how delightful this charming lady and accomplished actress was as Miss Moxon in "The Hobby Horse," and as Lady Betty Noel in "Lady Clancarty!"), Miss Blanche Horlock, Miss Fanny Brough, Mr. William Terriss, Mr. Mackintosh, Mr. T. N. Wenman, Mr. Albert Chevalier, Mr. J. H. Barnes, Mr. John Clayton, T. W. Robertson the younger, Mr. Brandon Thomas (in the days of "The Squire" playing as Mr. Brandon), Mr. A. Beaumont, Mr. Arthur Dacre, Mr. J. Maclean, Mr. Herbert Waring, Mr. George Alexander, Mr. Henley, Mr. J. F. Young, Mr. Charles Sugden, Mr. Hermann Vezin, Mr. Charles Cartwright, Mr. Charles Brookfield, Mr. Hendrie, Mr. Fuller Mellish, Mr. C. W. Somerset, Mr. R. Cathcart, Mr. H. Bedford, Mr. Webster, Mr. Lewis Waller, and Mr. H. Kemble. Yes, Mr. Hare was right. To one at least who remembers all these clever people and the excellent things that they did during the Hare and Kendal *régime* at the St. James's, it is a painful thing to write "Finis" to this chapter, and to know that so many pleasant and memorable evenings can only exist in memory.

CHAPTER IV.

THE GARRICK THEATRE.

1889—1895.

PENDING the completion of the Garrick Theatre in the Charing Cross Road, which was now being built for him, Mr. Hare accepted a brief engagement with Mrs. John Wood and Mr. Arthur Chudleigh, to create the important character of Jack Pontifex in Mr. Sydney Grundy's adaptation of the famous French farce " Les Surprises du Divorce," by MM. A. Bisson and A. Mars, entitled " Mamma." This was produced on September 24, 1888, the occasion being the opening of the new Court Theatre in Sloane Square, close to Mr. Hare's old theatrical home. The part was far removed from his accustomed line, and by playing it with marked success he proved his great versatility.   Mr. Percy Fitzgerald truly summed up the impersonation as follows :

" Mr. Hare has deservedly been praised for the spirit with which he played this part.   We can praise him more for the judicious reserve and the simulated earnestness he infused into it. Another would have been tempted into being rattling and boisterous, he was exactly the man he personated : 'natural, easy, affecting,' snappish at times, good humoured, and occasionally driven to frenzy.   This variety is found in nature, which is often, if not always inconsistent."

In the cast of " Mamma," which was an emphatic success, were Mrs. John Wood, Miss Filippi, Miss Annie Hughes, Miss Caldwell, Miss M. Brough, Mr. Arthur Cecil, Mr. Eric Lewis, and Mr. Charles Groves.

Mr. Hare's opening night at the Garrick (one of the most beautifully appointed houses in London) was April 24, 1889, the play Mr. Pinero's " The Profligate," heralded by the fateful lines—

" It is a good and soothfast saw :
 Half-roasted never will be raw ;
 No dough is dried once more to meal,
 No crock new shapen by the wheel ;
 You can't turn curds to milk again ;
 Nor Now, by wishing, back to Then ;
 And having tasted stolen honey,
 You can't buy innocence for money."

The event had been looked forward to with intense interest, and the handsome theatre was thronged by a brilliant audience that included the leading lights of the literary, artistic, and fashionable worlds. I need not in these pages say anything of Mr. Pinero's nobly conceived and finely written play, or of the acting triumphs achieved in it by Miss Kate Rorke, Miss Beatrice Lamb, Miss Olga Nethersole, Mr. Lewis Waller, Mr. Sydney Brough, and, above all, Mr. Forbes Robertson. With characteristic modesty Mr. Hare contented himself with the small part of Lord Dangars, and with consummate skill made it a great one. I have seen other and very capable actors play Lord Dangars, and the part has " gone for nothing." " The Profligate " was recognised as one of the best plays, if not the best, that had been seen for years, its success with that critical first night audience was beyond all doubt, and high though public expectation ran, it was everywhere felt that in every respect the production was worthy of the occasion.

In the July of this year Mr. and Mrs. Kendal left England to fulfil the first of their brilliantly successful professional engagements in America, and a "God-speed" banquet, at which the Right Hon. Joseph Chamberlain presided, was given in their honour in the Whitehall Rooms of the Hotel Métropole.

At this representative gathering Mr. Hare in the course of a very happy speech said— "Speaking in the name of the profession to which I belong, I can safely say that Mr. and Mrs. Kendal will carry with them to America the hearty good wishes of their brother actors and actresses, to whose regard and esteem they are entitled by long years of devotion to the best interests of their art, and by the possession of those social and domestic qualities which would have rendered them distinguished in any calling to which they might belong.

" I think our profession is singularly fortunate, inasmuch as, having survived, I hope to a great extent, those prejudices to which Mr. Chamberlain has alluded, and which once most unhappily surrounded it, it is now in touch —and in kindly touch—with all branches of society.

" Indeed, hardly a week passes but we receive some generous—I may almost say affectionate —token of regard from leading representatives in politics, in medicine, in law, and from the great brotherhood of other arts. We are proud of the interest our calling inspires, and we specially rejoice when any compliment is paid to those whose career in our profession has conspicuously adorned it. Such a compliment has this evening been paid to Mr. and Mrs. Kendal by the brilliant gathering assembled to wish them God-speed, great success, and a happy and speedy return from the great continent which they are about to visit for the first time. In consenting to preside at this banquet Mr. Chamberlain has added another to the long list of statesmen whom the cares and battle of politics have not prevented from taking a kindly interest in fellow-workers in a widely different field, who though players, perhaps still add their quota to the public good, and whose lives are no more free from anxieties and responsibilities than their own. I feel sure that in his future recollections Mr. Chamberlain will feel a pleasure in knowing that amongst the lighter duties which he has been called upon to perform, he will have performed no more graceful one than when he consented to preside at this gathering."

It soon became evident that in his new theatre Mr. Hare had no intention of reversing his old policy, and that it was more the desire to produce the best presentable plays in the best possible manner than to add to his long ago well-won reputation as one of the finest actors who had ever graced the English stage, that had induced him to re-enter upon the heavy cares of management.

It was while " The Profligate " was in the high tide of its first success that he set himself one of his most difficult tasks, the production of an English version of Mons. Victorien Sardou's " La Tosca," made famous in this country as well as in France by Madame Sarah Bernhardt.

The task of adapting this gruesome but fascinating drama was entrusted to Messrs. F. C. Grove and Henry Hamilton; and with a magnificence and perfection of scenery and appointments that excelled anything that even Mr. Hare had ever attempted, it was produced on November 28, 1889.

Well was it said on that occasion, "Mr Hare deals liberally with his public." For the principal characters he engaged Mrs Bernard Beere (who had the difficult task of following Madame Bernhardt as Floria Tosca), Mr. Forbes Robertson (who never did anything better than Scarpia), Mr. Lewis Waller and Mr. Herbert; while in comparatively small parts such distinguished artists as Miss Rose Leclercq, Miss Bessie Hatton, Mr. Gilbert Farquhar, Mr. Sydney Brough, and Mr. Charles Hudson were seen.

On the Parisian stage the drama had never been so richly or artistically mounted, and, taking it from "an all-round point of view," it had probably never been better acted. During the run of " La Tosca " Mrs. Bernard Beere unfortunately fell ill. At a very short notice her terribly exacting part was taken by Miss Olga Nethersole, and played by that young actress in such artistic and vivid fashion as to win the praise of the most critical.

The evening of February 22, 1890, should ever have some special mark in the theatrical calendar, for then Mr. Hare appeared for the first time in Mr. Sydney Grundy's remarkably clever adaptation of MM. Labiche and Delacour's " Les Petits Oiseaux," most happily called " A Pair of Spectacles." It would be a trite thing to say that everybody's friend, dear old Benjamin Goldfinch, is the best of Mr. Hare's unique collection of stage portraits,—but he has certainly never done anything better,—and it is one of those rare parts that an actor can go on playing until the end of his professional career. Fanciful stories that are at once witty

and purposeful, cannot grow old fashioned,—and
" A Pair of Spectacles " is exquisitely fanciful
and wholesomely purposeful. Does any one
grow weary of the delightful old fairy tales
that have lived through the passing fashions of
generations upon generations, and will go on
living through all ages to come? No! and
thank Heaven for it, they can never become
what smart playgoers, in order to show their
shrewdness, love to term " old fashioned!"
Although it is intensely human, there is about
" A Pair of Spectacles " the good old fairy-tale
ring, and so long as it is well acted (and indeed
it is a piece that requires the very best of acting),
it will assuredly hold the stage. Personally I
am inclined to agree with those who say that
Mr. Hare's Benjamin Goldfinch is the most
wonderful thing he has given us,—for here,
without any resort to artifice, he contrives to
completely change the nature and expression
of the man who alternately regards the world
and his associates through the medium of
sombre-hued and rose-tinted glasses. But
his acting in this part is beyond praise,—indeed

it is not acting, it is nature itself,—so cheery
and happy in his belief, so miserable while
struggling against his new-formed suspicions,
and once more so truly contented when, getting back his own spectacles that have been
mended, he with them recovers his belief in
goodness. It is not unusual to hear would-be
wiseacres say that the story of " A Pair of
Spectacles " is "improbable." Of course it is
improbable, and it is meant to be improbable.
Hans Christian Andersen's matchless fairy
tales, Charles Kingsley's " Heroes " and
" Water Babies," Richard Jeffries's " Wood
Magic," and to cite a stage subject, Mr. W.
S. Gilbert's " Pygmalion and Galatea " are all
beautifully improbable, but they will all live.
And as long as Mr. Hare chooses to go
on playing Benjamin Goldfinch, Mr. Sydney
Grundy's " A Pair of Spectacles " will live.
Equally good was, and still is, Mr. Charles
Groves's well dominated and inexpressibly
humorous rendering of Uncle Gregory, the self-
made, tight-fisted man, who " cooms fra
Sheffield " and sets everything wrong in his

generous brother's household. Nothing could be happier than the contrast between the methods of these two admirable comedians. In fact the whole production was one of those happy events that come to us "once in a lifetime."

During the first run of "A Pair of Spectacles" occurred the twenty-fifth anniversary of Mr. Hare's happy married life. This "silver wedding day" could not be passed over without recognition from his loyal and devoted associates at the Garrick Theatre, and by them he was presented with a beautiful set of George III. silver fruit dishes, and a right cordial letter of congratulation. In the same year (1890) his son Mr. Gilbert Hare made his *début* as a professional actor at the new Theatre Royal, Richmond (appearing in the bills as Mr. Gilbert Dangars), with a promise that has since been most satisfactorily fulfilled.

Like Lord Tennyson's perennial "Brook," "A Pair of Spectacles" seemed likely to "go on for ever," but engagements have to be kept, Mr. Pinero was ready with his new

·play, and, on March 7, 1891, " Lady Bountiful "
was produced.

For his text the author took these dainty
lines—

> " My masters, will you hear a simple tale ?
> No war, no lust, not a commandment broke
> By sir or madam—but a history
> To make a rhyme to speed a young maid's hour."

Now I am afraid that this was what the
playgoers of four years ago did not want.

Mr. Gilbert's 1885 " young lady of fifteen "
had just attained her majority, and she and her
parents did not want to listen to histories
written " to speed a young maid's hour," but
were inclined (and I think that subsequent
theatrical productions will prove that I am right)
to revel in hearing of broken commandments. I
think, too, that the young ladies who are fifteen
to-day will without undue restraint, be differently
influenced, for surely during the last year or
so their playgoing parents have had some more
or less startling stage experiences! We may all
be,—indeed I think we all should be,—very
sorry for the lady with a past. She may be

—and I doubt not very often is,—a very much injured lady. It is manifestly our duty to help the poor creature as far as in us lies. But on the other hand, we need not make her the heroine of romance, and permit our fifteen-year-old daughters to think that, from this point of view, she is pathetically ideal.

Be these things as they may (and after all they are not much more than matters of opinion), it is a pity that "Lady Bountiful" was produced (as I believe it was produced) at a time when "simple tales" were hopelessly out of fashion. One has only to read it to see what a beautifully conceived and admirably written work it is : one had only to see it to marvel at the manner in which it was placed upon the stage, and to be grateful for the good work done in it by Mr. C. W. Somerset, Mr. Forbes Robertson, Mr. Charles Groves, Mr. Gilbert Hare (who now made his first appearance at his father's theatre), Miss Carlotta Addison, Miss Kate Rorke, Miss Dolores Drummond, Miss Marie Linden, and Miss Caroline Elton. Mr. Hare played the

splendidly drawn character of Roderick Heron,
—a gentleman who, according to Mr. Pinero
(the best of authorities on the subject), was a
very near relation of the immortal Harold
Skimpole. This clever and unflinching impersonation might alone have made the success
of the play,—in which all the stage pictures
were realistic to a degree, and the interior of
an old church remarkably beautiful.

Of course "Lady Bountiful" attracted a vast
number of appreciative playgoers, but I shall
never think that the production met with the
merit that it deserved,—and I feel certain that
playgoers have themselves to thank for making
Mr. Pinero realise that he need no longer
cater for "masters" who were supposed to
want a "simple tale."

On September 19, 1891, Mr. Hare gave
the highly interesting revival of "School"
of which I have already spoken.

On January 2, 1892, he produced Mr.
Sydney Grundy's absorbing play "A Fool's
Paradise," which had already been seen in
London at a Gaiety matinée, and, under the

title of "The Mouse Trap," in America. In this Mr. Hare gave an admirable study of the shrewd, cynical, but good-hearted physician,— Sir Peter Lund. Astute and caustic, yet kind and considerate, quick in snubbing an impertinence, yet very gentle and urbane to those he loved, Mr. Hare was in every phase of a difficult but thoroughly telling and well-understood character supremely excellent. He gave his audiences a picture of the fashionable, clever physician who, whilst ever ready to gibe at the follies of those around him, does not hesitate to administer like rebukes to himself and his own profession. To quote a well-known critic: "The character of Sir Peter Lund certainly deserves a place 'on the line' cf Mr. Hare's gallery of portraits." Prominent in the cast of " A Fool's Paradise " were Miss Kate Rorke, Miss Olga Nethersole, Mr. F. Kerr, Mr. H. B. Irving, and Mr. Gilbert Hare. On the same evening Mr. Hare produced a pretty one-act play adapted from the German by Mrs. Bancroft, and entitled " My Daughter."

It was not for twelve months that Mr. Hare required a novelty, and then he appeared,—on January 5, 1893,—as Valentine Barbrook in Mr. R. C. Carton's charmingly conceived but all too slender play, " Robin Goodfellow." Mr. Hare's character was not an agreeable one, but he played it to perfection. "Mr. Hare," said a critic, " is faultless as Valentine Barbrook. Make-up, business, rapid alternations of sham *bonhomie* and hard, sharp, cruel villainy,—sticking at nothing in the interests of self—are all admirable. The man lives. We feel that ' we know that man ' as we watch him hoodwinking his poor old mother, alternately bullying and cajoling his daughter, tricking the ingenuous young lovers, and scattering broadcast the seeds of misunderstanding and misery. Valentine Barbrook is an unpleasant creation, but none the less a brilliant one from the critical standpoint."

And to this let me add the testimony of Mr. William Archer, who is nothing if not critical, and who says :

" Mr. Hare's Valentine Barbrook is a de-

lightful piece of acting, which would lend
attraction to a much duller play than ' Robin
Goodfellow.' It is not the first character of
the same type which Mr. Hare has presented
to us ; but the beauty of the thing lies in the
delicacy of its differentiation from its pre-
decessors."

The revival of " Diplomacy," which was
the attraction that succeeded " Robin Goodfellow," was in every respect a happy thought.
Messrs. Clement Scott and B. C. Stephenson's
singularly adroit adaptation of Mons. Victorien
Sardou's " Dora " is always likely to be
popular ; and when it was announced that in
it Mrs. Bancroft would make her reappearance
after her temporary retirement from the stage,
general delight was expressed. So great,
indeed, was the interest felt in this production,
that before the first performance the advance
booking exceeded two thousand pounds a
week. On the evening of February 18, 1893,
the brilliant audience at the Garrick included
the Prince and Princess of Wales, the Duke
of York, the Duke and Duchess of Fife, and

all the leading members of aristocratic, artistic, and literary circles. At the largely attended reception on the stage that followed the performance, a presentation of a watch-bracelet of diamonds was made to Mrs. Bancroft by Lady Jeune on behalf of the Princess Christian. This was the gift of a number of ladies,—old friends and admirers of Mrs. Bancroft's,—who wished to give definite expression to the pleasure with which she was once more welcomed on the stage. The cast of " Diplomacy" was a remarkable one. Mr. Forbes Robertson and Miss Kate Rorke were the Julian Beauclerc and the Dora,—the parts so splendidly played on the original production of the piece by Mr. and Mrs. Kendal. Miss Olga Nethersole and Lady Monckton appeared as the Countess Żicka and the Marquise de Rio-Zarés. Mr. Bancroft and Mr. Arthur Cecil resumed their original characters of Count Orloff and Baron Stein. Mrs. Bancroft was the Lady Henry Fairfax, Mr. Gilbert Hare the Algie Fairfax, and Mr. John Hare appeared for the first time as Henry Beauclerc.

No wonder that "Diplomacy" was enthusiastically received, and that, both in London and the country (where with all these famous artists it was subsequently taken), it had a long and prosperous run.

This and the productions to which I shall now briefly allude, are too fresh in the minds of the playgoer to need any detailed comment on my part.

On January 6, 1894, Mr. Hare appeared as Julius Sterne in Mr. Sydney Grundy's original five-act comedy, "An Old Jew;" and on April 7 of the same year as Major Edward Hardy, R.A., V.C., in "George Fleming's" four-act play, "Mrs. Lessingham." Both were powerful character studies, well worthy of his name and fame. As Julius Sterne, with the piercing eyes, keen grey face, long white hair, and velvet skull-cap he was fascinatingly picturesque, and he invested the portrait with an air of mingled shrewdness and benevolence that was eminently pleasing. There was a pathetic dignity, too, in the patient composure with which he bore the fierce reproaches of his son until the inevitable moment when other lips than his revealed the cruel secret of his life, that was appreciated by all who can understand true art.

As the worthy Major Hardy, Mr. Hare acted with no diminution of his well-known sincerity, decision, and firmness of touch. In speaking of this life-like impersonation Mr. William Archer said : " Major Hardy gave Mr. Hare another chance of proving the versatility of his art. The character is a delightful one, and Mr. Hare played it delightfully.   It does not come within what we are accustomed to consider Mr. Hare's 'line,' but the mistake lies in supposing that so accomplished an actor is tied down to any 'line' whatever." " Mrs. Lessingham " was followed by a revival of " Caste," in which Mr. Hare relinquished his old part,—Sam Gerridge,—to his son Mr. Gilbert Hare, and to the disappointment of his friends, did *not* appear as Eccles.

Then followed another notable and highly popular production of " Money," with Mrs.

Bancroft as Lady Franklin, and Mr. Hare as
Sir John Vesey. The revival brought back to
the memory of frequenters of the old Prince of
Wales's, and the reconstructed Haymarket
under the Bancroft reign, many agreeable
reminiscences. It was like a vision of those
cheerful playgoing-days, to meet with Mrs.
Bancroft once more enacting Lady Franklin
with that incomparably honest laugh and merry
twinkle of the eye which have never served her
better than in the character of the gay and
frolicsome widow. Mr. Hare's Sir John Vesey
was not less happy in its associations, and it was
a pleasure to find his performance even more
remarkable than of old for that firmness of
outline and that effective colouring which he is
able to impart to this typical portrait of sham
geniality and restless self-seeking.

The cast,—which included Mr. Arthur Cecil
as Graves, Mr. Charles Brookfield as Captain
Dudley Smooth, Mr. Forbes Robertson as
Alfred Evelyn, Mr. Arthur Bourchier as Lord
Glossmore, Mr. Kemble as Stout, Mr. Gilbert
Hare as the old club member, Miss Kate Rorke

as Clara Douglas, and Miss Maude Millett as Georgina Vesey,—was a notable one, and once more Lord Lytton's fifty-year-old play drew the town.   In the autumn of the year the character of Georgina was very charmingly rendered by Miss Helen Luck.

Mr. Hare commenced his 1895 campaign with the production of Mr. Sydney Grundy's "Slaves of the Ring."   This did not prove a fortunate venture, but whatever the faults of the play might have been, it at least afforded Mr. Hare an opportunity for adding one more remarkable portrait to his already well-filled gallery of eccentric old men.   In make-up, voice, and gesture his impersonation of the lame, half-deaf, half-blind Earl of Ravenscroft, who, although regarded as a painful example of senile decay, uttered more clever things in his queer imbecile way, and showed a shrewder judgment of character, than any other member of his little circle, was inimitable, and the most wonderful thing about it was that in every respect it differed from the previous pictures of old men Mr. Hare had given us.

" When in doubt play trumps !" That is the immortal piece of advice given to the uncertain whist player, and that is what Mr. Hare did when, finding it necessary to provide an early successor to " Slaves of the Ring," he revived " A Pair of Spectacles." It came at the right time, at a moment when the English stage had been over-inundated by so-called problem plays, and when playgoers wanted a change ; and so once more old Benjamin Goldfinch was made right royally welcome. Who could wonder at it ? As Mr. Clement Scott pointed out, " A Pair of Spectacles " is " one of the very best adaptations of a French original that has ever been presented to the stage since George Henry Lewes, John Oxenford, and Tom Taylor reproduced French plays ; and not only does the public delight in the work, but the old students of the stage applaud it, and not one of the new students of the stage has one word to say against it."

" A Pair of Spectacles " more than held its own until Mr. Pinero's remarkable play, " The Notorious Mrs. Ebbsmith," was ready, and Mr.

Hare made his latest, and in some respects his greatest, acting success as the elderly rake and would-be peace-maker, — the Duke of St. Olphert's.

It is in this cleverly conceived and superbly portrayed character that Mr. Hare elects to make one of his first appearances before an American audience. The success of Mr. Pinero's powerful play in London is of too recent date to call for comment in these pages.

But Mr. Hare's friends and the public wanted to see him once more as Benjamin Goldfinch and Lord Kilclare, before he bade a temporary farewell to the Garrick Theatre ; and accordingly on June 15, 1895, the last night of his season, " A Pair of Spectacles " and " A Quiet Rubber " were performed to a crowded, expectant, and sympathetic audience. Mr. Hare has never encouraged the practice of making managerial speeches before the curtain, but on this occasion it was obviously impossible for the popular actor and manager to avoid a few words of farewell. And so at the close of an admirable performance, and having been enthusiastically received, he said :

" I am aware that in certain quarters there exists a strong prejudice against an actor-mana-ger taking the liberty to address an audience in his own theatre ; but even by the most pre-judiced it will not, perhaps, be denied that there are occasions when not only is no excuse needed for such a step being taken, but that it is actually incumbent upon him to say a few words to his audience. To-night I feel, ladies and gentlemen, to be such an occasion if ever there was one, for I feel that I cannot allow you to leave this theatre without, in the first place, thanking you for the compliment you have paid me in being present here, and the hearty sympathetic manner in which you have followed the performance of these two old plays. It would be affectation if I attempted to be ignorant that the increased cordiality you have shown this evening is to a large extent due to the place which I believe I have the honour to hold in your regard, and as significant of your good wishes to an old servant of the public who

is about for a time to leave you. To-night it is
my sad task to bid you farewell for many, many
months ; indeed, I cannot definitely fix in my
own mind when I may next have the honour of
appearing before you. I go to try my fortunes
in the great American continent with the hope
of making fresh friends amongst those who have
always shown such encouragement, generosity,
kindness, and sympathy to English artists. If
I fail there, I shall at least know that the fault
is only mine, for I have had every hope held
out to me that a friendly welcome will be
extended to me, and to those who accompany
me. I hope to make my appearance in New
York in the same programme I have presented
to-night, and I shall have in it the support of
Mr. Groves, 'the only Gregory,' my son, and
other members of the company, with the exception, I regret to say, of my old friend Miss Kate
Rorke, who has been with me since I opened
this theatre. For the presentation of Mr.
Pinero's play, 'The Notorious Mrs. Ebbsmith,'
I have secured the services of Miss Julia
Neilson and Mr. Fred Terry ; and I am in

formed that their first appearance in New York
is being looked for with the keenest interest.
During my absence in America, and beyond it,
I have been fortunate enough to secure as a
tenant, Mr. E. S. Willard, who will open his
season with a new play by an American author,
and I am sure will have the good wishes and
hearty support accorded to him which are justi-
fied by his great reputation and distinguished
talent, and that he will receive a warm welcome
when he makes his bow on this stage before you.
It only remains for me, my dear friends, to say
goodbye, and to thank you, as the public, for
the support and indulgence accorded to me for
upwards of thirty years; for your more than
generous appreciation of any good work which
I may have done ; for your indulgence and
forbearance with my many shortcomings. I
wish, also, publicly to thank the Press for the
help, kindness, and encouragement it has accorded to me from the time of my first appearance in London till the present moment ; and
lastly, the members of my company, past and
present, who have ever rendered me loyal and

devoted service never to be forgotten. I hope in a new country, ladies and gentlemen, to make new friends, but my heart must ever be with my old ones, with that generous English public to whom I owe, indeed, everything, and whom I shall remember in my wanderings with feelings of the utmost gratitude and affection."

CHAPTER V.

IF by this time I have not shown my readers that Mr. John Hare is the most modest of men my little biography must be badly written. By the way, I suppose that in this "personal" chapter I ought to mention that his name is really John Fairs. Following the custom of the days when he tentatively sought his fortune on the stage, he adopted an assumed name and winning success under it, wisely retained it for himself and the members of his family. It was emphatically the right thing to do, for in the history of dramatic art the name of Hare must always live. My record of Mr. Hare's achievements clearly shows that his modesty has never stood in his way, and, indeed, it is certain that true modesty, backed by invincible energy, and that wonderful capacity for taking pains which is the true definition of genius, helps rather than retards a man's career; but it is wonderful to know, as I do, how little, after his thirty years of arduous and splendidly successful stage work, he thinks of himself and his histrionic triumphs.

He knows, of course, that he is beloved by his family and intimate friends, that he is the eagerly sought companion of his large circle of acquaintance, and that his name is a familiar one in the play-bills and in the newspapers. But he does not know how well known, both on the stage and off, he is to the thousands and thousands to whom his supreme art has given infinite instruction and lasting delight.

And yet, in an odd way, this was once brought home to him. One evening on leaving an evening party, to which he had accompanied Mrs. Hare, he walked some distance down the long carriage rank looking for a " four-wheeled cab." To his annoyance he was followed by one of those objectionable London "touts," who, running beside him, kept touching his forehead, and in the slimily obsequious fashion of his tribe, saying, " Kerridge, my lord ? Kerridge, my lord ? May I get your lordship's kerridge ? "

At last Mr. Hare, having silently ignored his persecutor, secured his conveyance, and was on the point of driving home, when the persistent one, putting his head through the window, said, " Where to, my lord ? " Now Mr. Hare can be emphatic as well as modest, and on that occasion he incisively remarked, " Oh ! go to the devil !" Whereupon, thrusting his face and his lantern into the cab, the touting linkman, with an altered manner and an indefinable grin, said quietly, " Business still keepin' pretty good, I 'ope, Mr. 'Are ? "

Mr. Hare tells me this as a humorous incident in his experiences, but the fact is, that the cab tout was one of the many thousands who, all England over, know him both in and out of the theatre, and honestly rejoice to know that " Mr. 'Are's " business is good !

No doubt the fact that he has for so many years almost exclusively played old men's parts has left a very confused idea in the public mind with regard to his age, a fairly general belief existing that he might be "anything between eighty and ninety."

On many occasions this not wholly unpardon-
able blunder on the part of people not acquainted
with him or stage history has caused him considerable amusement.   In some of the provincial newspapers that have recorded his
performances in small towns, where he has
not been well known, he has been told that
" considering the age of the veteran actor " his
success has been " most noteworthy."

An early instance of this mistaken identity
occurred when he had only been eighteen
months on the stage.   It was during the *furore*
caused by the success of " Society " that, getting
into a carriage of the underground railway, he
unexpectedly found himself face-to-face with an
old school-fellow whom he had not seen for some
years.   Not knowing that he had adopted the
stage as a profession, and taken the name of
Hare, his friend cried out, " Hullo ! Fairs, how
are you ? " and after they had chatted about old
times, the conversation turned to the theatres.
He asked Mr. Hare " if he was fond of the
stage ? " and having received a reply in the
affirmative, presumed that he had " been to the

Prince of Wales's to see 'Society,' the piece of which everyone was talking." "No," said Mr. Hare, doubtfully, "I can't say that I have *seen* it." "Then you should go at once," said his friend. "It's a capital play, and a devilish clever old man acts in it, a fellow named Hare."

Another of the many instances bearing on the same point is as follows. It occurred at a time when Mr. Hare was still quite a young man, but had made himself famous by playing old men's parts.

He was on the look-out for a good English terrier, and happened to mention the fact to a friend of his, who was also his solicitor, and he told him that one of his articled clerks was a great dog fancier, and had an animal of the kind for sale. Now this young gentleman, it appeared, was not only fond of dogs but of the theatre, and being an appreciative playgoer, had enrolled himself among the most ardent admirers of Mr. Hare. "I know," said the solicitor, "that it would please him very much if you would let him bring the dog and show him to you." To this Mr. Hare readily assented, and a day or so later he was roused from his bed early in the morning by the announcement that a gentleman had called, and was waiting in the dining-room "with a dog." Hastily dressing, Mr. Hare hurried down, and found a very young gentleman, and a dog that was not in any way what he wanted. To his annoyance, too, he noticed that as they discussed the question of the dog the young gentleman's manner was supercilious and patronising, not at all the sort of thing that he should have expected from " one of his greatest admirers." And so, making the interview as brief a one as possible, he made some polite excuse for not purchasing the dog, thanked its owner for the trouble he had taken in the matter, and bade him good day.

Subsequently his solicitor friend told him that on his clerk's return he asked him if he had satisfied his desire and seen Mr. Hare, and if he had sold the dog.

" No," said the young gentleman, "I have been terribly annoyed. The old man was in bed and sent the young one down to me."

This of course accounted for the flippant manner that had irritated Mr. Hare, who at that time was twenty-five years of age!

But the oddest of all these incidents (and there have been any number of them) occurred during the first run of " A Pair of Spectacles." Mr. Gladstone, always keen to discover and appreciate true art, had from the very outset of his career been one of Mr. Hare's warmest admirers, and soon after the production of Mr. Sydney Grundy's clever play, and accompanied by Lord Rosebery, he came to make acquaintance with Benjamin Goldfinch. At the conclusion of the performance he had a long talk with Mr. Hare with reference to the play and other matters On similar occasions the actor had talked with the great statesman, but it had almost always happened when he was made-up for the stage. Shortly after this interview his wish to meet him in private life was gratified, and he sat with him at the dinner table of a mutual friend. Most of the guests present were known to Mr. Gladstone, but during dinner he inquired of his hostess the

names of those he had not met before. Looking in Mr. Hare's direction, he asked; "Who's
that?"   "Mr. John Hare," was the reply.
"Oh! yes, yes," said Mr. Gladstone, "I know
his father, the manager of the Garrick Theatre."
In a conversation between the two that took
place later in the evening, Mr. Gladstone
laughed over his mistake, and "discoursed,"
says Mr. Hare, "with his usual charm and
knowledge, on acting, and on actors, past
and present."

Apropos of Mr. Gladstone's marvellous power
of observation the following little story of him
in connection with "A Pair of Spectacles" is
very interesting. As those who are familiar
with the play will remember, most of the
characters in it—the wife, the son, the friend, the
butler, and the bootmaker, in all of whom
Benjamin Goldfinch has placed his implicit
trust and absolute belief—gradually become,
through the influence of the malign spectacles
of Uncle Gregory, objects of distrust and
suspicion. In the end, however, Goldfinch is
disenchanted, and one by one, and each in turn,

the characters re-reveal themselves to him in their true light as worthy objects of trust and affection. The scheme of the author is, in the first and second acts, to demolish each of Goldfinch's objects of belief, and in the third act to restore them. Never yet was play produced that did not require alteration, and on the first night of " A Pair of Spectacles " it was discovered that the scene in the third act, where the bootmaker places himself in his proper light, dragged the play, and (as Mr. Hare felt), at the expense of the logical development of the story, it was ruthlessly cut out. It was hoped that no one would notice this change, and no one did until Mr. Gladstone saw it and said, " A charming play! The only thing that struck me was that where such great ability had been shown in its construction, and where wife, son, friend, and butler are permitted to re-establish themselves in Goldfinch's eyes, it seems a pity that the bootmaker should not have his opportunity." The keen eyes of Mr. Gladstone were the first, if not the only ones, to detect the flaw.

That Mr. Hare has the enviable gift of

making and retaining close friendships goes without saying. Of his earliest stage friend, Leigh Murray, he always speaks with affectionate gratitude, and I may jot down here two stories told him in the early Liverpool days by that once famous artist.

On the occasion of the first appearance in London of his old friend Sims Reeves in the character of Edgar Ravenswood, Murray went to Drury Lane. He was then quite a young man, very particular with regard to his dress, and exceedingly careful as to his personal appearance. On the same evening he had been acting in an opening play at the Adelphi Theatre as a raffish young gentleman who was compelled to pawn his watch, and in the course of the piece he had to produce the pawn-ticket from his waistcoat pocket. Now this waistcoat was a smart white evening one which, as it was quite suited to his visit to Drury Lane, he, in order to save time, kept on. On his arrival at the theatre he deposited his hat and overcoat in the cloakroom, and at the conclusion of the performance he found himself, while waiting his turn to reclaim his property, the centre of observation of a group of unknown admirers, who in him had recognised that certain source of attraction —a popular actor. Not a little pleased at this, Murray, with a self-conscious air, and a pardonable little bit of swagger, produced what he believed to be the cloak-room ticket from the fateful pocket, and said, "My hat and coat, please." The attendant, with a broad grin, returned the ticket, saying, "I think there is some mistake, sir." Alas! it was the property pawn-ticket, and poor Murray's chagrin and mortification may be imagined.

The other story belongs to theatrical history. The famous comedian Fawcett was a special favourite with George III. The King took the greatest interest in him and his performances, and on many occasions honoured him with kindly recognition. Fawcett lived at Slough, and had received the royal permission to walk when he chose in the private grounds of Windsor. On one occasion he had for his guest a fellow actor named Cooper, and in company with him he took advantage of the privilege the King had given him. On their

walk Fawcett suddenly saw his Majesty un-
accompanied and approaching them. " Here
comes the King," he said to his companion.
" He will probably speak to me, and while he
does so you had best drop back a little."
" Ah!" said Cooper, " what would I not give to
be spoken to by the King!" "Well," replied
Fawcett, " he'll see you with me, and perhaps
he will speak to you." The King approached
and, in his well-known way of repeating the
same word twice over, thus addressed the
favoured comedian. "Well, Fawcett Fawcett?
How are you, Fawcett Fawcett? What was
the piece last night, Fawcett Fawcett?" "' The
School for Scandal,' your Majesty," replied
Fawcett. " Capital!" said the King ; and so for
a few moments the conversation went on. At
last, noticing Cooper, the King said, " Who's
your friend, Fawcett Fawcett?" Upon which
Cooper slightly advanced. "Mr. Cooper of our
company, your Majesty," said Fawcett, as
Cooper bowed low. " Ah! yes, yes!" said the
King; "I know, I know! Very bad actor,
very bad actor!" This was how poor Cooper

realised his ambition, and was spoken to by George III. ! "

It was when " Ours " was tentatively produced in Liverpool in 1866, that Mr. Hare made lasting friendships with many members of the Bar, notably with Mr. Charles Russell (afterwards Sir Charles Russell, and now Lord Russell of Killowen, the Lord Chief Justice of England), Mr. R. McConnell, Mr. Aspinall, Mr. (afterwards Sir) John Holker, Mr. Leofric Temple, Mr. W. S. Gilbert (then a briefless barrister), and many others. Of course, Mr. Hare has been, and is, a distinguished as well as a highly popular member of the leading literary and artistic London clubs. Of the Garrick Club he has many cherished recollections. " I was admitted a member of this club," he tells me, " in (I think) 1868, and in it I have made some of the best and dearest friends of my life. I was proposed by the late Frederic Clay,—most accomplished of musicians, and most agreeable of men ; and I was seconded by Val Prinsep. What memories are associated with the many years of my membership of the Garrick ! On

my first introduction to the card-room, I found
to my delight that amongst its frequenters and
whist-players were (I take the names at random
and as they occur to me) Anthony Trollope,
Charles Reade, Charles Lever, John Millais,
Henry James (now Lord James of Hereford),
and occasionally James Clay, the finest whist-
player in the kingdom, and who deserted the
higher points of the Turf Club and the
Portland (where he was accustomed to play),
to meet his friends at the Garrick, and join in
the modest ' shilling ' points which are there the
abiding law.   I remember well with what awe
and reverence I stood behind the great whist-
player's chair to take in my early lessons of the
king of games !   Curiously enough, on the very
first of these experiences, Mr. Clay revoked,
and to see such a thing as that has not, I take
it, fallen to the lot of many men !   With what
kindness, what hospitality, what sympathy with
the young, is the name of James Clay associated
in my mind !   In my early London days I was
a frequent guest at his table, and very memorable are those Sunday dinners of his, strictly

limited with regard to number, but generally comprising some of the most interesting and talented people of the day. In my early Garrick days, a characteristic story was current concerning Charles Reade and Henry James, who were partners one afternoon at the whist-table. Charles Reade, one of the largest hearted and kindest of men, was extremely 'touchy,' and stood very much on his dignity. Upon this occasion he happened to pause a very long time before playing out a card, and this induced from Henry James the friendly remonstrance, 'Now then, old Cockeywax, fire away!' Knowing Reade's peculiarities the other players were anxiously silent, and were not surprised when, at the end of the rubber, Reade with great ceremony rose and left the table and the room, ominously declining to play any more. This caused Henry James great distress, as of course nothing was further from his thoughts or wishes than to intentionally offend Charles Reade. Accordingly, when they met on the following day, he went up to him to express his regret that annoyance had been felt at what

2

was meant as a mere piece of chaff. 'I don't like chaff,' said Reade, in his severest manner, 'and I strongly object to being called old Cockeywax.' 'But,' said James, 'you are mistaken. I did not use the word. I did not say old Cockeywax, but old Cockeylorum.' 'Oh!' said Reade, with a gleam of humour in his eye, 'If you said old Cockeylorum, that makes all the difference, and we can shake hands and say no more about it.' This story Lord James told me himself. It was in these days that my friendship with John Millais began, a friendship strengthened and cemented by years, and by my increasing and intimate knowledge of the most simple, most large-hearted and most delightful of men. Neither success nor the honours that have been heaped upon him by his own and other countries have in the remotest degree spoilt that fine and manly nature. As John Millais was to his friends in '65, so he is in '95. I recall a story of him that is characteristic. Just after he had been created a baronet, and on entering a room in the club where a few of his old and intimate friends were sitting, he was received with shouts of welcome and congratulation mingled with a good deal of good-natured chaff. This pleasant banter lasted a considerable time, when at last Millais said, ' It's all very well for you fellows to chaff, but you don't know what a baronetcy does for you. I have had an experience of it within the last day or two. I was asked by the committee of the Manchester Autumn Exhibition to go down to " hang " for them, and on arriving there I went to an hotel and addressed the very charming young lady presiding in the office. " I want a bedroom and a fire, if you please," I said ; and she, turning from me brusquely, went to the speaking tube, and called up it, " No. 325 and a fire," and then, addressing me, said, " What name ?" I replied " Sir John Millais," upon which she beamingly returned to the tube, and called, " No. 27 and a *good* fire ! " '

" Whether this was due to the dignity of the title or to the still greater honour associated with the name of Millais will never be known.

" I shall always feel that the greatest com-

pliment ever paid me was Millais's desire to
paint my portrait. 'I'm going to paint you,
old fellow,' he said, 'and you must come and
sit for me next Sunday.' I went again and
again, and charming indeed are the recollections
of those sittings, of his bright and cheery talk,
and the infinite pains that he took with his work.
When the picture was finished he, with characteristic generosity, presented it to my wife, for
her lifetime and my own, with the understanding
that it shall ultimately become the property of
some National collection, to be named by him."

It was at the Garrick Club that Mr. Hare
entertained the Daly company to supper on the
occasion of their first visit to London. For
this notable event permission was given by the
committee to use the large dining-room.—a very
special privilege. Between eighty and ninety
sat down to supper, and Mr. Hare recalls with
gratification how his chief guests of the evening,
"the clever Americans who had so delighted us
with their acting," sat down in the presence of
the portraits of their great histrionic ancestors
with which the walls of that famous room are

hung. Altogether the evening was a very great success, and several excellent speeches were delivered ; " two particularly graceful ones," says Mr. Hare, " being by my guests, Mr. John Drew and Mr. James Lewis."

This seems a fitting time to enumerate those who met at the Garrick on this most interesting evening.

The Daly Company was represented by Mr. John Drew, Mr. James Lewis, Mr. George Clarke, Mr. Otis Skinner, Mr. Bond, Mr. Charles Leclercq, Mr. F. Grove, and Mr. Holland.

Amongst those present to meet them were : the Earl of Lathom, the Earl of Cork, the Earl of Londesborough, Right Hon. Sir Henry James, Q.C., M.P. (now Lord James of Hereford) ; Sir E. Lawson, Bart. ; Sir Richard Quain, Bart. ; Sir John Millais, Bart. ; Sir Frank Lockwood, Q.C. ; Sir Arthur Sullivan, Sir Charles Hall, Q.C. ; Sir Henry Irving, Hon. Lewis Wingfield, Mr. L. de Rothschild, Mr. H. Lawson, M.P. ; Mr. E. Dicey, C.B. ; Mr. Maclean, Q.C., M.P. ; Mr. Montagu Williams,

Q.C. ; Mr. Phelps (United States Ambassador);
Mr. W. S. Gilbert, Mr. A. W. Pinero, Mr.
Clement Scott, Mr. Sydney Grundy, Mr. H.
Herkomer, R.A. ; Mr. S. B. Bancroft, Mr.
Luke Fildes, R.A. ; Mr. W. H. Kendal, Mr.
J. L. Toole, Mr. Bret Harte, Mr. Wilson
Barrett, Mr. Henry Abbey, Mr. Beerbohm
Tree, Mr. W. Winter, Mr. Henry James, Mr.
Corney Grain, Mr. E. Terry, Mr. John
Hollingshead, Mr. Henry Neville, Mr. D.
James, Mr. J. Comyns Carr, Mr. G. Broughton,
R.A. ; Mr. Parkinson, Mr. A. Critchett, Mr. J.
Knight, Mr. C. W. Mathews, Mr. T. Thorne,
Mr. C. E. Perugini, Mr. A. Cecil, Mr. A. Levy,
Mr. Bendall, Mr. Welch, Mr. A. Watson, Mr.
G. Hare, Mr. E. Crabb, Mr. Weldon, Mr.
Cathcart, Mr. Godfrey, Mr. Chitty, Mr. Du
Maurier, and Dr. Playfair.

Mr. Hare also cherishes fond recollections of
the Arundel Club, of which he became an
invaluable member soon after his first appearance in London.

" It was," he says, " the most delightful of all
Bohemian gatherings, and the good-fellowship,

good humour, and bright wit that ruled our
meetings will be recalled by all who can remember them. Amongst the constant frequenters
of the Arundel in those days, were Talfourd,
Tom Hood, Henry S. Leigh, Prowse, Tom
Robertson, H. J. Byron, Arthur Sketchley,
Artemus Ward, W. S. Gilbert, Clement Scott,
Joseph Knight, and last but not least, Peter
Hardy, for many years our Honorary Secretary,
and endeared to every member of the club by
his genial and affectionate disposition. Most of
these have, alas! joined the majority, but one
and all were the 'princes of good fellows,' and
their names are associated with all that is bright
and clever."

Then there was that unique little *coterie*
whimsically self-styled " The Lambs."

" This delightful little club," says Mr. Hare,
" was started in 'the sixties,' and I may claim to
have been its part founder. It consisted of
twenty-four members, the first twelve being
called ' The Lambs,' and the second twelve
' The Lambkins.' The chairman was ' The
Shepherd.' We had no regular club-house,

but met for many years at the Gaiety Restaurant, and subsequently at the Albemarle Hotel. 'The Shepherd' wore a badge, and called 'attention' by means of a silver bell mounted on a crook. The object of the club was simply fun and good fellowship, and right royally it achieved its ends. It was a rule that only two speeches should be made : the one by 'the Shepherd,' who proposed any subject he chose, and called upon any member he thought proper to respond to it. As he invariably chose the man least acquainted with the subject in question, great fun ensued. Amongst the original members were S. B. Bancroft, Henry Irving, Harry Montague, Charles Santley, Charles Collette, Sir Douglas Straight, Henry Tufton (now Lord Hothfield); and Lord Newry (now Earl of Kilmorey).

"The club prospered for many years; a surprising number of years, indeed, considering the small number of its members. As an instance of our freedom from superstition, and our justification in our common sense, I may mention that at the 'Annual Washing,' generally

held at Skindle's Hotel, at Maidenhead, we, on
four consecutive occasions, sat down at the ill-
omened number of thirteen to dinner, and that
during that period we did not lose one of our
comrades. I believe I am correct in stating that
when poor Harry Montague, one of the most
popular of our ' Lambs,' settled in New York,
he founded the ' Lambs' Club ' that has since
been so popular in that city."

The " Two Pins Club," which was an institu-
tion of much more recent date, is another
pleasant memory. It was originated by Mr.
F. C. Burnand and some of the members of
the *Punch* staff, its object being that its
members should from time to time meet on
horseback, ride out to some London suburb,
lunch, and return together. It was named
the " Two Pins " by the editor of *Punch*, in
honour of the immortal memory of John Gilpin,
and the members were expected to combine
the fearless horsemanship and the amiable disposition of that redoubtable equestrian.

"At the time I speak of," says Mr. Hare,
" Lord Russell of Killowen was its President,

F. C. Burnand (its founder) the Vice-President, and amongst its strictly limited number of members were Sir Edward Lawson, Sir Frank Lockwood, Sir John Tenniel, Linley Sambourne, Harry Furniss, C. W. Mathews, R. Lehmann (the honorary secretary), and myself. These little meetings were very delightful, and were the source of much welcome fun and good fellowship. On one of our expeditions an amusing incident occurred. One of our members, whom I will call X., was riding by the side of Sir Frank Lockwood, our route being Wimbledon Common and its vicinity. To the amusement of those present X. was full of rather far-fetched reminiscences of the district. 'Ah! how well I remember this place when I was a boy,' he said, 'and how changed it all is! Where that church stands I shot my first snipe, and many and many a brace of partridges have I knocked over near the dear old windmill. In that white house yonder, hospitable old Tompkins lived; and where that row of cottages now stands was a pretty field where I flirted with the parson's daughter.'

"At this moment Sir Frank Lockwood, whose eye was twinkling with humour, caught sight of a distant shop sign-board bearing the legend 'General Stores.' No one but himself had noticed this, and, turning to X., he said, 'Oh ! by the way, old fellow, did you happen to know General Stores in those days ?' 'Oh dear, yes !' promptly replied X., 'he is a very old friend of mine, but at that time he was only a captain.' That from that day to this X. has been mercilessly chaffed about his old friend 'Stores' may be easily imagined, but it is only fair to add that he has borne it in the best of good temper, and like the fine fellow that he is."

One of the first friends Mr. Hare made when he commenced his acting career in London was Mr. J. M. Levy, the editor and proprietor of *The Daily Telegraph*. From the first he showed him welcome encouragement and the greatest personal kindness,—and his friendship never varied from the time of their first meeting to the day of his death. For many years, Mr. Levy kept what might almost be called "open house" to his wide circle of friends, and at his table and receptions were to be found the leading representatives of Art, Literature, and Society. Sunday evenings at his house were things to be remembered ; Patti, Nilsson, Albani, Trebelli, and, indeed, all the great singers of the day, contributing to make these delightful gatherings memorable.

As a loyal Englishman Mr. Hare naturally recalls with pride the gratifying occasions on which he has had the honour of acting before the royal family.

At Sandringham, by the desire of the Prince of Wales, he gave a performance of "A Pair of Spectacles," on the birthday of the late Duke of Clarence,—the last birthday, alas ! that the young Prince lived to see. The Prince and Princess of Wales took the greatest interest in this entertainment, keeping it a secret from their son in whose honour it was given. Mr. Hare had a special act-drop prepared for the occasion, showing white satin curtains, and cupids holding a wreath with the inscription, "Many Happy Returns of the Day." The Prince, the Princess, and the Duke, were greatly pleased with this "happy thought," and the whole performance was received with enthusiasm. The Prince of Wales, the Duke of Clarence and others joined the Garrick company at supper, and before he left, and although he was in his travelling dress prepared for his journey to London, the Princess insisted upon Mr. Hare's presence in the drawing-room, where in her own gracious manner she most cordially received him.

A week or two after this performance Mr. Hare was summoned to Marlborough House by the Prince of Wales,—who received him in his study, spoke in the most eulogistic manner of the entertainment, and presented him with a beautiful silver cigar-box. This was decorated on the outside with the Prince's crest and motto in gold and enamel,—and (also in enamel) the head of a hare wearing gold spectacles. In the inside, in a fac-simile of

His Royal Highness's handwriting, was the following inscription :

" To John Hare (Fairs)
from
Albert Edward, P.

In remembrance of ' A Pair of Spectacles
at Sandringham, 1891."

The happily conceived detail of this most interesting souvenir was entirely the invention of His Royal Highness, and is one of innumerable proofs of his infinite thought and kindness.

The commands that Mr. Hare has had the honour to receive to appear before the Queen were both most interesting experiences, although strangely contrasted.

The first was at Windsor Castle, where " A Pair of Spectacles " was given. This might almost be described as a " Performance of State," as all the Court ceremonials were strictly enforced. The representation took place in the Waterloo Chamber, and did not commence until nine o'clock. The room was beautifully decorated, and prior to the perfor-

mance Mr. Hare was consulted by the Princess
Louise with regard to many details likely to
tend to its success, and especially with reference to such arrangements as would enable
the Queen to see and hear properly. To this
end a short trial was given on the stage, and
the acoustic properties of the room thoroughly
tested. In front of the stage, and screening
the orchestra, was a superb bank of ferns,
palms, and flowers, and as Her Majesty suffers
greatly from the effects of over-heated rooms,
large blocks of ice were deftly used to equalise
the temperature. At nine o'clock the Court
took their places. The Lord Chamberlain
and the other members of the household wore
their official dresses,—officers were in full
uniform, and when to these were added the
handsome dresses and the sparkling diamonds of
the ladies, the scene was as impressive as it
was beautiful. Shortly after nine the orchestra
played the National Anthem, and, preceded
by the Lord Chamberlain and followed by the
Lords and Ladies in waiting, the Queen
entered. Immediately the Court rose and

remained standing until Her Majesty was seated and the performance began. As Court etiquette at Windsor forbade any excessive demonstration on the part of the audience, the reception of the comedy was necessarily quiet, and at first rather trying to actors who had been accustomed to the more enthusiastic expressions of approval in a public theatre. But, apart from this, the Queen makes a thoroughly " good audience,"—being both appreciative and critical. She has always taken the liveliest interest in the theatre, and never fails to remember the names of the favourite actors of her youth,—a fact amply demonstrated when, during recent years, their descendants have sometimes appeared before her. On the occasion of Mr. Hare's appearance at Windsor his company included Mr. R. Cathcart (his stage manager) and Miss Lizzie Webster. When, after the fall of the curtain, he was sent for by Her Majesty, she asked him if it was the same Mr. Cathcart whom she had seen acting with Charles Kean, and if Miss Webster was the grand-daughter of Benjamin

Webster? On learning that in each case her surmise was correct, she expressed much interest. Mr. Hare and his company were received at Windsor with more than kindness, and were treated with consideration never to be forgotten.

In the autumn of 1893 Mr. Hare received the Queen's command to appear at Balmoral in " Diplomacy," at that time being played by him with Mr. and Mrs. Bancroft, and the Garrick company in Scotland. Here was a striking contrast. At Windsor a State Performance before the Empress Queen with all the pomp and ceremony of the Court. At Balmoral all homely and informal. No ceremony ; no state ; Court etiquette on the part of the audience entirely set on one side; no restraint placed upon applause; and the reception of the play as enthusiastic and exhilarating as if it had been acted before an appreciative holiday audience. At Windsor Mr. Hare was received by the Queen as the Queen ; at Balmoral by the Queen as a lady in her own private house. To the actors the evening was made doubly memorable

by the presence in the audience of the Empress
Eugénie. Since the death of the Emperor
Napoleon it was the first time she had been
present at a theatrical performance, and she was
profoundly interested and moved. At the reception subsequently given by the Queen in the
drawing-room she was present, and Mr. Hare,
Mr. and Mrs. Bancroft, Miss Kate Rorke, and
other members of the company had the honour
of being presented to her. She conversed a
great deal with them, and it was touching to
note her revived interest in the artistic pleasures
from which she had been so long and so sadly
separated. On this occasion the Queen specially
honoured and pleased Mr. Hare by command-
ing Mrs. Hare and his daughter to witness the
performance, and to be presented to her at the
reception by which it was followed.

Shortly before supper (which was attended
by the members of the Royal Family and the
Court) the Queen retired, but she still continued
to take the liveliest interest in the proceedings,
and Mr. Hare has since learnt that she sent
down from time to time to ascertain if the

"players" were "well bestowed." After supper
Mr. Hare's health was proposed by Prince
Henry of Battenberg, and before leaving
Balmoral each member of the company was
given a beautiful souvenir in the shape of a
handsome brooch to the ladies, and a scarf pin
to the gentlemen. These were presented by
the Princess Beatrice in the name of Her
Majesty. In addition to a magnificent silver
cup given to Mr. Hare, the Queen sent him a
few days later a full-length engraving of herself
after the portrait by Angeli, signed in her own
hand, " To Mr. John Hare from Queen Victoria,"
together with a most kind letter from her Groom
in Waiting, the Hon. Alec Yorke, expressing the
great delight she had felt in witnessing the performance of " Diplomacy."

Mr. Hare's Scotch tours are not always associated with this spirit of generosity. Like other
managers travelling with expensive companies,
and producing their plays in the country as
perfectly with regard to scenery and appointments as if they were being acted in London,
he is compelled to make a small increase in the

ordinary provincial admission prices.   This is a
thing that some people loudly resent, and in
passing, I may mention that it is a curious fact
that those who on such occasions talk of
"extortion," and write to the local newspapers
concerning their alleged grievances, seldom or
never patronise the theatre and support its
manager when good dramatic fare is offered at
the customary rate.   They belong to that very
large class who want the very best of everything
at something very much below its market value.
Well, playing in Dundee the other day, Mr.
Hare heard of a man who wanted to go and see
him act but who was very wrath, when with his
wife he presented himself at the pit entrance, to
find that the usual shilling seat was advanced to
eighteenpence.   "Well," said the sympathetic
friend to whom he angrily told this terrible story
of London rapacity, "of course you didn't go
in ?"   "Oh yes," the canny Scot had "gone
in," but he *sent his wife home,* and so through
Mr. Hare's greed had *put sixpence in his own
pocket !*"

It was at Dundee, too, that the following

incident occurred. As a first piece, Mr. Theyre Smith's dainty comedietta, "Old Cronies," was being played (and capitally played) by Mr. Gilbert Hare and Mr. Charles Groves. The play is a duologue, devoid of dramatic action, and depending entirely on its clever dialogue and repartee. A frequenter of the pit, who expected the two actors on the stage to exhibit some of the dexterity and physical prowess associated with the "Two Macs," had sat the piece half way through in patience, when suddenly his temper gave way, and he yelled out in such broad Scotch that I shall freely translate it here, "Now then! Where's my eighteen-penny-worth! Why don't you begin your BUSINESS!"

Then there was a curious incident at Edinburgh. Mr. Hare had reached that part in "A Pair of Spectacles" where Gregory has succeeded in instilling into Benjamin's mind distrust of everybody and everything, and has even suggested that Mrs. Goldfinch's attendance at church is associated with a *penchant* for the curate. Left alone at this crisis Benjamin says, "Gregory has not improved of late. He grows surly and suspicious, but if he thinks that because Buzzard's an impostor, I am going to suspect everybody, even my own wife, he is mistaken." Whereupon a man in the gallery shouted out, "Well done, old un! Stick up for the Missus!"

In a way these impromptus are entertaining enough, but to the actor they are as disconcerting as the unrehearsed effects which, in spite of all care, will now and then make themselves all too prominent, and which are far more likely to occur on the bustling provincial tour than in the methodically conducted London theatre.

Mr. Hare, for example, is not likely to forget one night when he was playing in "A Quiet Rubber," and had come to the end of the great quarrel scene between Mr. Sullivan and Lord Kilclare. On the offended old Peer's reappearance to leave the "parvenu's" house for good, it is necessary to bring on to the stage a small portmanteau. This was given to him as usual by his servant. Now it is also necessary when touring that all the luggage should be labelled in a special manner. On his entrance with the portmanteau (a pathetic little incident that should be and almost always is received in hushed silence), Mr. Hare was amazed to find himself greeted with tremendous shouts of laughter, the meaning of which he could not for the life of him understand. But on turning the portmanteau round to pack " Ireland under Elizabeth," and " The Noble Families of Galway," he saw pasted on its side a large label with the words, " MR. JOHN HARE'S GARRICK THEATRE COMPANY, MANCHESTER." Then he grasped the situation.

That Mr. Hare's pre-eminently refined style is thoroughly understood and appreciated in English provincial towns is an established fact, and the man who went to see him the other day in " A Pair of Spectacles," at Bradford, and in his broad Yorkshire dialect said, " I thowt it rot ! A' dunno wot's coom to Thayter Royal. Thar's been na' good moorder ' thar' for last six moonths ! " is one in a million.

On the first visit of the Comédie Française

to London (it was in those terrible days at the
end of the Franco-German war and the
Communist riots in Paris, and when their own
theatre was closed to them), Mr. Hare had the
opportunity of making the acquaintance of many
of its most distinguished members.   It com-
prised in those days, Got, Delaunay, Bressant,
Sarah Bernhardt, Favart, and many other
brilliant artistes, and his meetings with them are
amongst his most cherished recollections.   He
was a member of the committee formed. to
consider what steps should be taken to pay
some special compliment to these distinguished
visitors, and he was of course present at the
famous luncheon that was ultimately given in
their honour at the Crystal Palace.   " The
desire to meet our famous guests," he says,
" was so great that we had much difficulty in
limiting the numbers, and a very important
point was the selection of a chairman.   At last
this narrowed itself between Lord Dufferin
and Lord Granville, both fluent French
scholars, a very necessary consideration as the
proceedings had to be conducted in French.

Finally it was decided to ask Lord Dufferin to preside, and accordingly I accompanied my good friend, Mr. Joseph Knight (the excellent Honorary Secretary of the committee), to Lord Dufferin's house to personally ask him to accede to the wishes of the committee. At once and in the kindest manner he expressed his delight in accepting the position. The affair was a supreme success, and the sight was one of the most brilliant and extraordinary I have ever witnessed. I suppose on that day, the sun shone through the transept of the palace on as great a number of distinguished men as had ever been gathered together. On the right of Lord Dufferin sat Got, on his left Bressant. Then came Lord Granville and others according to precedence. The scene was curiously picturesque. According to their custom our French guests wore evening dress, and Bressant to ward off the rays of the sun threw a table napkin round his head. Always an aristocratic and distinguished looking man, this curious head-dress seemed in an odd way to lend additional dignity to his face and figure, and he

looked "the noblest Roman of them all."
Admirable speeches were made by Lord
Dufferin, Lord Granville, and Mr. Alfred
Wigan, and these were responded to by Mons.
Got, the *doyen* of the great French company.
After dinner we had coffee and cigars on the
terrace, a portion of which had been reserved
for our use. Our guests were full of life and
spirits, Delaunay especially displaying the gaiety
of a school boy out for a holiday. What a
contrast to his impressive acting as Perdican in
'On ne badine pas avec l'Amour,' which we
saw at the Opera Comique Theatre that night!
By all who had the good fortune to see him on
that occasion it was agreed that he had never
played more finely."

Speaking of the increase in the actor's
remuneration that he has lived to see, Mr.
Hare tells me : " I received £5 per week for
performing Sam Gerridge at the old Prince of
Wales's Theatre. Many years afterwards,
when 'Caste' was produced at the Criterion,
Mr. Charles Wyndham offered me £100 per
week to reappear in it, but my other engage-

ments prevented my accepting this flattering proposal."

Of course this is very satisfactory, and no one rejoices more than Mr. Hare that dramatic art should at last be properly recognised and rewarded ; but he is not wholly in love with the state of things that exists in the stage-land of to-day.

Especially he deplores the fact that the rawest of amateurs are not only permitted to appear on the stages of important theatres, but, what is worse, are in far too many instances accepted by the thoughtless and the ignorant as genuine actors. "A musician or a singer," he emphatically and very rightly maintains, "if he dared to appear on the platform before he had studied and to some extent mastered his art would be hissed back into obscurity. But in English theatres so-called actors are allowed to 'do their exercises' in the very presence of those who presumably pay to see finished acting."

Unluckily this is only too true. Only the other day, an estimable lady told me that she was certain her son would be able to make an enormous success on the stage because he "had such a good memory," and would so easily "learn his parts." If the mere "learning of a part" were all that is necessary for the equipment of a successful actor, who would not take to the stage! The unfortunate thing is that amongst average audiences there are so many who cannot discriminate between the self-satisfied parrot and the true artist. Considered from the art point of view the actor's calling has been and presumably always will be thus heavily handicapped.

That Mr. Hare's ideal is a high one goes without saying, and in connection with it I may quote his own words:*

" If an actor's imagination suggests nothing beyond what he has succeeded in producing, if, in short, he is completely satisfied with what he has done, there is something radically wrong

---

* NOTE.—These views were for the most part communicated to a representative of the *Birmingham Daily Gazette*, and were embodied in an article that appeared in that journal under the title of " Mr. John Hare on Acting."

with his artistic constitution. Impersonations have their history, their life, their growth and progress to a degree of perfection within the confines of an actor's powers. And a time comes when a character is, so to speak, in its zenith, when the actor can do no more, and then, if he be not careful, decadence sets in. Characterization is an art, and like music or literature, it demands a right temperament, an inclination, bent of mind, a fund of talent, and natural genius. Without this necessary stock-in-trade the actor is an impossibility. And, even granted this capital, this artistic nature, which must be inborn, and cannot be induced or acquired, nothing will avail its possessor without an immense amount of energy and hard work. What some people call the inspiration of the moment I heartily distrust. Genius is essentially sane, and subject to the laws of sanity; it does not break free from all rule, but is tractable, and grows from strength to strength with ripening experience. There is a legend of some grand passion which comes upon the actor in the evening and transforms the character he has

not taken the pains to bring before the mind's
eye in moments of solitary reflection into something sublime and wonderful. Robson, they tell
me, was this order of man, an artist who never
became his part until he was rapt with the
glamour of the footlights. I remember Robson
well, and I tell you plainly I don't believe it.
Jefferson, Irving, Coquelin, Got, students every
man of them, have relied on study, not on the
chance excitement of the moment, which, though
it may stimulate an actor to a great and successful effort, is much more likely to lead him astray
from the paths of probability and nature. The
character is assumed by the actor, but does not
displace his own identity. He does not lose
himself in the part, but retains a critical self-
consciousness ; he experiments and watches the
result ; he reasons out the meaning of the
spoken words, and when a new interpretation of
any point occurs to him, he notes its effect in
practice with the closest attention. Imagination
is his light, and reason his guide. Many of
these emendations are failures, no doubt, and
often, starting on a wrong premiss, the actor

finds himself landed in a fallacy. Then the
advice of a brother craftsman is invaluable. He
is an unwise man who shuts his mind against
the hints of a colleague. Those who see from
without can discern many things that it is impossible to discover by any criticism from
within.

"So art progresses, and in the course of years
undreamed-of possibilities reveal themselves to
the view. This it is that makes the early training of the actor of so much importance. Why is
it that acting seems so easy to the novice, and so
difficult to the man of experience? The reason
is that where the one only sees a simple idea
the other beholds a complex problem, which only
concentration of mind and imaginative sympathy
can enable him to compass and present in a
logical form. Owing, however, to the unfortunate position of the drama in England
raw youth has to drag through its novitiate in
public."

Mr. Hare is strongly in favour of the French
Conservatoire system, but says:

"Not that acting can be taught as bootmaking

and tailoring are taught. That is out of the question. But granted the artistic temperament, that necessary capital I spoke of before, the preliminary training (without which one cannot arrive even at journeyman rank), may be learned just in the same way as the technics of music or painting. If these elements of the art were taught by a master the public would be spared the melancholy spectacle of some sorry wight floundering about on the road of incompetency. Many an unsuccessful actor would be saved the humiliation of exposure and public derision, and men and women of talent would be able to go on the stage armed with the confidence that only comes of knowledge. But the uninitiated of to-day, unable to walk properly, ignorant how to bear themselves properly, and utterly unable to manage their voices, must learn this rudimentary lore of the craft in the full blaze of the theatre. Is it not obvious that the experience of men like Samson and Regnier, Coquelin and Got, must be of the greatest possible value to a beginner? It is very well to have the capacity to feel, but what will it avail a man if he does not know how to make use of the machinery of expression, gesture, and intonation, by which feeling is conveyed to others ? On the stage alone do people challenge criticism in their art before they have grasped its elements."

Hoping that this brief chronicle will find American as well as English readers, I have asked two kind American friends of mine, Madame de Navarro (Miss Mary Anderson), and Mr. Bret Harte, to tell me what they think of Mr. Hare's art.

Madame de Navarro writes me :—

" DEAR MR. PEMBERTON,

" I am delighted to hear that you are writing an account of Mr. John Hare's past work. I feel quite certain that when the American public see him they will place him where he should be placed—among the few great artists of our time.

" The first time I met him was at dinner at our mutual friends the Kendals. I sat next to him, and continually wondered at his resemblance, in looks, voice, and manner, to my famous countryman Edwin Booth. Shortly after this I went to see him act, expecting him to impersonate the kind of parts taken by Booth. I was therefore greatly surprised to find him playing a character in which his make-up so disguised him that the Booth resemblance had entirely disappeared. He had, in fact, become a little ruddy-faced old gentleman who kept the audience beaming with pleasure from the beginning to the end of the performance. His acting reminded me of the best French school; so excellent in its numberless and nameless *nuances;* so perfect in its art! The late Lord Lytton (Owen Meredith) once said to me: ' John Hare, by virtue of the delicacy and beauty of his work, belongs to the Théâtre Français. Most people appreciate and admire it, but I fear that many of its charming touches escape the middle-class English eye.' *I* think he belongs to humanity at large, for he is so finished in his work, so great in his simplicity, and so *true to nature* that his art must appeal to all classes, and to all nationalities.

" With a thousand good wishes for the success of your work,

" I am, yours most truly,

" MARY ANDERSON DE NAVARRO."

Mr. Bret Harte writes me :—

" MY DEAR PEMBERTON,

" If anything is to be written of John Hare introductory to his visit to America, I am delighted that it should fall to hands as appreciative and conscientious as yours; although, it seems to me scarcely possible that so accomplished an artist as he should require any other introduction to my countrymen than the 'bill of the play' and the lifting of the curtain. For to see him act is to love him, and 'to love him is a liberal—theatrical—education.' I know that America will be quick to recognise that while he is in tradition and experience thoroughly an *English* actor, he expresses that finest quality of restraint so beloved of the Comédie Française, but which we here don't always recognise in the highly emotional *rôles* it sends across the Channel to us. What I think is still more remarkable in Hare's acting is his complete abnegation of self in his characters—a quality so strong that it seems to heighten the efforts of those who support him ; he is *the character*, and the others are capital *actors* who exist to *draw him out*.   I don't believe that applause ever startles him from this singular and delightful concentration.   I have seen him come before the curtain to receive his well-earned tribute with a slightly pained and deprecatory air, as of one who should say, 'You really *mustn't* praise me for acting, you know ; it's the other fellows.   I am really Mr. So-and-So !'   It is for this reason—*because* he has made the whole scene so delightful, and put everybody at their best, that one is apt to forget *him* in the perfection of his art, and one does not always yield him his full meed of applause.

"I am told that he takes with him to America a limited *répertoire*, and that it is likely to affect his popularity with the masses.   I should not predicate that of a people who have made Jefferson immortal in one or two plays !—and he is quite as fortunate in his 'Pair' of Spectacles' as Jefferson was in his 'Rip van Winkle.' What a wholesome breath is wafted over the footlights in Grundy's charming adaptation of that pretty French trifle? I do not believe that we, in America, are so familiar with the miasma of cynical doubt, or the fire-damp of explosive sentimentalism, as to draw back in our stalls from so honest and re-vivifying an atmosphere. And how delightfully Hare, even with look and gesture, traces the unfailing optimism of the hero, through its momentary refraction and aberration into cynicism under the distorting lens of the bor-rowed spectacles, to the perfectly natural and convincing climax! One such play, and one such character, should carry him far across the Continent and far into the hearts of the American people,—and I shall be much mis-taken if they do not.

"I am not a critic—Heaven forfend!—so I cannot approach his art properly equipped and consciously superior. But I should like to dwell on what seems to me to be his singularly crisp delivery,—every word ringing out clearly, so that even in his wonderful rendering of an old man's utterance, his mumble is never unintelligible, or his loquacity slurred or indistinct. His enunciation of emphasis is nearly perfect. I have a very vivid recollection of his delivery of the apology forced from Spencer Jermyn by his wife in the last act of 'The Hobby Horse.' The language is very simple—as Pinero always is when he is most subtle—so simple I should hesitate to transcribe it, but Pinero knew that Hare could inform it with the very spirit of the irony he intended. So that it stands now with Hare's delivery, as one of the most delightful and sarcastic *résumés* of the moral and sentimental situations of a play I ever witnessed.

"It seems to me also that so much could be said of his wonderfully minute study of the half senile character, where the habits and impulses of youth remain to override the actual performance. There is a notable instance of this in his wonderful portrayal of the Duke of St. Olphert's in 'The Notorious Mrs.

Ebbsmith.' He is gallantly attempting to relieve Mrs. Thorpe of the tray she is carrying, but of course lacks the quickness, alertness, and even the actual energy to do it, and so follows her with delightful simulation of assistance all over the stage, while she *carries it herself*, he pursuing the *form* and ignoring the performance. It is a wonderful study! And who does not remember Beau Farintosh in ' School,' and all that splendid forgetfulness of the alas ! all too necessary eyeglass.

" Do with this what you like, only don't make my arms seem to ache with reaching up to pat such a tall fellow as Hare on the head !

" Yours always,

" BRET HARTE."

Before concluding this chapter I wish to record my sincere thanks to all the good friends who have helped and encouraged me in my work, and to many unknown friends from whose criticisms I have freely culled.

Of John Hare personally I could write much

more, but I know that he would be the first to cry " Hold, enough ! "

No one understood him better than his early friend and fellow worker, T. W. Robertson. Among that gifted but short-lived writer's papers were found some jottings of a comedy that he hoped to write for the Prince of Wales's Theatre. It was to be called " Passions," and Hare was to impersonate " Pride." It is easy to understand the sort of pride that Robertson had in his mind's eye, the proper pride that ennobles art, and does so much to make the single-minded man, the loyal friend, and the true gentleman. If poor Robertson had lived to write that part, he would indeed have fitted John Hare to a nicety.

THE END.

BRADBURY, AGNEW, & CO. LD., PRINTERS, WHITEFRIARS.